ZODIAC LOVERS

Paranormal Romance

Book Five

CETUS ✳ OPHIUCUHUS

LANCE TAUBOLD

ISBN-10: 0997791241
ISBN-13: 978-0997791242

DEDICATION

IN CETUS: FOR ED: WHO WOULD HAVE THOUGHT THE "STRAIGHT" GUY WOULD BE MY VERY OWN MUSE…

IN OPHIUCHUS: FOR RILEY: THANKS FOR LETTING ME USE YOU AS MY INSPIRATION. YOU MADE A GREAT ROMANCE HERO.

TABLE OF CONTENTS

CETUS

Cetus—The Whale

Traits: Luck (good or bad), Having to do with the mother, concerning the subconscious, Pertaining to the underworld or magic, or how they will travel by sea.

"Ahoy there, matey!" Captain Ransom St. James grinned broadly, greeting Clinton Porter, Clint to his friends, as he stepped off the ramp onto the Windjammer.

Clint's medium-brown eyes met the black ones of the most handsome and sex-exuding man he'd ever seen. The Captain appeared to be in his thirties. Tall. Teeth: brilliant white. The smile: big and genuine. Face: perfectly sun-burnished, a light five-o'clock-shadow—making him even swarthier. Hair: short, cropped, black. And that body! No shirt. A broad chest with a dusting of dark fuzz, even broader shoulders tapered in a V to a tight waist any body-builder would envy. He wore white board shorts, a stark contrast to his tanned physique. Muscled calves led to a white pair of deck shoes.

Devastating.

Clint's eyes traveled back to the perfectly formed chest then down the light treasure trail over the blocked abs and into the waistband of the white shorts. Clint hoped he wasn't drooling as he quickly shut his mouth, realizing it hung agape. This was his first gay cruise—his first cruise period—and his friends had told him the Windjammer cruises in the Caribbean were the best. Small. Intimate, and usually had the hottest guys. Well, they were right. This man before him was the hottest guy. And if he wasn't gay, Clint was going to jump overboard right now.

The exquisite hunk of masculinity still smiled and held out his hand, obviously used to the once-over Clint had given him. "I'm Captain Ransom St. James at your service. And who might ye be, my handsome fellow?"

He spoke like a romance hero—a pirate of the high seas. His gaze was piercing, intense... almost unnerving. "I... I'm Clint," he finally managed to stammer. He took the man's hand. "A pleasure." Understatement.

"The pleasure's mine." Ransom squeezed Clint's hand hard and held it, his eyes still locked on Clint's. "I'll be savin' a spot at the Captain's... er, my table, if ye'd like."

OH MY EFFING GOD! He'd been here two minutes and the most incredible man on the planet had just asked him for... well, kind of... a date. Next to him. At his table! Could this get better? Clint still clasped Ransom's hand. He feared if he let go his knees would collapse.

"I am correct in assuming you're here alone, Clint?"

"Ye... I mean, you are. It's my first time." Then quickly added, "On a cruise."

Ransom showed his pearly whites again and squeezed Clint's hand again. "Of course. Then I'll be doin' my best to make sure you have an adventure you will never forget." A final squeeze.

"I hope so." Clint squeezed back.

"Now Charley here will show you to your cabin." He motioned to his right.

Clint glanced right, and not six feet away way was a young, blond, thin—but nicely toned—man of twenty-one or so. Crap. I didn't even notice him. He's cute, but no Captain Ransom St. James, that's for sure. Who was? He must've heard the whole interchange between us. Too late now.

Charley grinned. "This way, Clint. Your bags are already in your cabin. I guess you'll be seeing the Captain at dinner." He turned on his heel and led the way.

Clint followed.

"Aye, you will, Clint," the rich baritone said to his back as he followed Charley down the deck. "Cocktails are served at 7:00 on the stern."

Clint smirked. Cocktails indeed. A dream cruise.

The boat or ship, whichever—Clint could never remember the difference between the two—wasn't big. It accommodated forty to fifty passengers, depending on the number of singles.

Clint had gotten a cabin—stateroom?—with a small patio. His friends said it was a must. Even it cost a little more he would be happy he had. Now looking around the smallish room, he was glad he had. His friends were two for two. Opening the door, he could look straight through the room to the patio at the back. Bright light poured in and made the room seem larger. He pictured himself with Ransom, drinks in hand, watching the starry night sky. Whoa! Dial it back, Clint. Here he was an hour into his trip and he was picking out the matching linens! He just wanted to have a good time, drinking, dancing... a little sex, nothing too complicated. He didn't expect to find the love of his life here. But... that would be okay too.

Clint stood out on his patio/balcony, looking out at the azure water. It had to be close to 5:00; they should be departing soon. Drinks… and Ransom at 7:00. Ah yes.

He stripped off his T-shirt and stretched his arms to the sky, taking in a huge gulp of the salty air. "I will not say, 'I'm king of the world.' I won't… not yet anyway. Maybe I'll read a bit and take a nap, get ready for my first night." He'd heard he probably wouldn't get much sleep on the trip. But if his waking hours were filled with the dashing Captain St. James, who needed sleep?

He had never had a burning desire to be married or be with someone forever. He'd had several relationships, most of them successful. None of them had ended with a bang or any real drama. They'd all kind of turned into friendships, which was fine. He was still friends with some of them and would occasionally hook up with one of them. But… he was going to be thirty-five soon—March 14th to be exact. Three weeks away. And while he still looked good, he thought—gym, good diet, moisturizer daily, not too much sun just healthy tan—time ticked on. He'd never had a problem getting guys. But like he told himself now… but. His contemporaries were all in— or looking to be in—long-lasting relationships or marriages. Life in L.A. was for the young—very young—and there were more of them "young 'uns" arriving all the time.

It was all starting to get old. And for the first time… lonely.

Being an A.D., assistant director, had afforded him a great lifestyle. He was good at his craft and worked as much he wanted. He had all of his industry friends, but he'd started to feel that if he left the business, no one would really miss him. That's L.A. for you:

friend of the moment. But he wasn't like that, never had been. He really counted his friends as friends, but the more he'd been thinking about it recently, he realized he was the one who was always making dates and plans. He wanted some reciprocation.

So he'd come on this trip to do some—ugh—soul searching. He hated that phrase, but that's what it was. He needed to figure out what he wanted to do with the rest of his life and where he wanted to be. He wouldn't be telling any of his fellow travelers what he did. He didn't want the "glamor" of Hollywood to influence them. He would be Clint from Pierre, pronounced "peer," South Dakota, who had a heating and cooling business with his dad.

He had a buddy Mike from college who had that background. Mike wouldn't mind. Where was Mike anyway? They'd been hot and heavy all through school. And Mike had one of the tightest, ripped bodies he'd ever seen, as well as being and all-around good guy. He never should have let that one go. But Mike hated UCLA and L.A. in general. It wasn't for him. So he took his degree in directing—and he was a good director—and headed back to Pierre, promising Clint they'd keep in touch. For a while they had. At least Mike had. Clint had tried his best too, but things were always coming up and he'd gotten caught up in the not-calling-back black hole of Hollywood. Then he rationalized that they were young and in college. It couldn't be anything serious, and with all the hot actors and wannabe actors in L.A., it should be easy to find someone as good and hot as Mike. Wrong. He hadn't found anyone better. Don't get him wrong, there'd been a smorgasbord of hot guys, each one more egotistical and vapid than the next. Mike was genuine. Down to earth. The real deal. No wonder he'd hated L.A.

The one that got away…

He hoped Mike had found someone good who made him truly happy. Maybe he'd call him when he got back. Why was he thinking about Mike anyway? Captain Ransom: He seemed real, and down to earth as well. Oh come on. You only met him for five minutes. But there was something… beyond overt lust. Time will tell.

He opened his suitcase and fished out a book. *Moby Dick*. He'd tried reading it a few times but just couldn't get through it. Maybe it wasn't the most appropriate book for the trip, but it was better than a Peter Benchley classic like *The Deep*, or *Jaws*, or even *The Island*. That was the modern day pirate one right? Like his piratey Captain Ransom St. James. He needed to stop obsessing. He reached into his suitcase again and produced another, slimmer book: *The Third Hour*, a religious thriller that he'd heard was quite good and very cinematic. Hmm. Maybe he'd try that first instead of tackling the six-hundred-plus-page tome. "God or the whale?" he said aloud. "Ah well, let's give the whale another shot."

An hour and a half later he awoke and rushed around trying to get ready for cocktail hour. He hadn't meant to fall asleep, but the sea air and thirty pages of Ahab and Ishmael had been the perfect sedative. The dinner would be casual dress he knew from the itinerary. White linen shorts (not too wrinkled), a pale yellow T-shirt, docksiders, his blond hair fashionably messy: he was ready to go. He looked good. More importantly, he hoped the Captain would think so. He was growing excited at seeing him again.

He looked once more in the mirror on the back of the bathroom door. "You're like a teenage girl going on your first date. Dial it back, boy." He pointed at his reflection. "Ransom St. James, here I come."

The dining room was on the main deck, but the bar and cocktails were on the upper deck. Clint was glad there were only the three basic decks. He knew big cruise ships had many decks and it took take quite a while to traverse them. This was easy. He needed easy. He eagerly, but not too eagerly, made his way along the narrow corridor to the steps to the upper deck. He didn't want to be sweating when he sat down. And God forbid he had pit-stains for the next couple of hours. He strolled in the lounge and saw a few guests already sipping their libations.

"Right on time. I like that. I'm so accustomed to everyone being fashionably late on these cruises."

Clint couldn't prevent himself from jumping a little. The Captain had just popped up at his side.

Ransom smiled a dazzling smile, trying to hide his mirth. "I didn't mean to startle you, Clint." He put a hand on Clint's upper arm and Clint almost jumped again from the heat coming from it. Heat that quickly traveled south.

Clint found his voice. "I didn't expect you to be here. I mean, so soon."

"I have to greet my guests. And I find a drink or two doesn't hurt, either, with these cruises."

More men started arriving and Clint moved out of the way to let them in. Ransom turned slightly to his left and produced two coconut-shaped mugs with some sort of frothy concoction in them. That's when Clint noticed the ever-efficient Charley standing there standing off to Ransom's left, the obvious warden of the concoctions.

"Thank you, Charley. Two more in ten minutes please… unless of course you see we've finished them sooner." Ransom turned to Clint. "You'll find they're quite intoxicating and delicious."

Clint noted Charley had disappeared. "They look delicious. What are they called?"

A glint came into Ransom's eyes. "Captain's Ransom. My special drink. The ingredients are an ancient secret. Cheers."

"Cheers," Clint rejoined, and took a sip. "Woo. It is delicious… and strong." He took another sip and let the tart, yet vaguely sweet, mixture slide down his throat. The froth on top tickled his lips and made them tingle.

"May I?" Ransom leaned into Clint and flicked out his tongue on Clint's upper lip.

Clint stopped breathing. Had that just happened?

Ransom's tanned face reddened. "I'm very sorry, Clint. You had some froth on your lip… Forgive me. That was unbelievably rude and incredibly forward. I've never… I don't know what came over me. You remind me of someone I knew long ago. He… never mind. It's not important. If you wish to leave me, I will understand. I have no excuse."

Clint smiled at Ransom's discomfiture. *He's adorable and not arrogant in the least. Who do I remind him of? An old boyfriend?* "Well, Captain—"

"Ransom. Please."

"Ransom. You do come off pretty strong, but I can't deny I'm attracted to you. And we are on this ship for only a few days. It's not like we can date. I'm sure this is how you've probably operated on other cruises. I didn't really think I'd find my lifetime companion on a—"

"Clint, please stop." Ransom looked completely chastened—even a little hurt. "I have undoubtedly given you a wrong—and bad—impression of me. This is not the way I "operate," as you put it. I have never come on so strongly to someone I was attracted to before. I cannot give you a logical explanation for my behavior. It was nothing you said or did. It was simply you. There is something about you—your essence—that attracts me. And I lost control." He smiled devilishly. "Of course. You are incredibly attractive physically as well. But if you could forgive me, I would like to start afresh." He winked. "Court you properly."

Clint's eyebrows raised. "Court me properly? Could you be more charming? There's nothing to forgive. You've explained yourself perfectly." He took a big swig from the coconut mug. "I do like the courting idea, though. On the other hand, we do only have a few days. And I know you have other guests and duties to attend to. Any time you have to spare for me will be great."

"Thank you for being so gracious for my rudeness. I am the

captain, however. I have a good working crew and the guests usually take care of themselves. With those things in my mind, I am as available as you want me to be. In other words, Clint…" He took Clint's free hand in his. "I'm all yours."

Now Clint didn't know what to say. This incredible man had just offered himself up on a silver platter to him, and he wanted to feast. He took another large gulp of this drink and emptied it. Before he could take another breath, a new one magically (Charley) appeared in his hand and the empty vanished. "Charley is amazing… and pretty cute. Why haven't you—"

"He's my first mate. And while incredibly efficient—and cute—he is not my type, as well as complicating matters." He stared directly at Clint. You have not responded to my offer."

Clint took a too large gulp of his new drink. Here goes. "I would like to take you up on your offer, but with the stipulation that if you do have duties or commitments or something you'd rather do, you'll do them and not worry about me. I'm a big boy." He sipped again, noting that his head was getting a little cloudy. He'd better watch it.

"Accepted." Ransom squeezed Clint's hand, which he still held firmly in his, then pulled him in close. He stared deeply into Clint's eyes and slowly moved his lips to Clint's, parting them slightly.

"More froth?' Clint whispered.

"No."

And their lips met.

Clint's head spun—but not from the alcohol—as his lips

parted and Ransom's tongue met his. The "Captain Ransom" drink was nowhere near as intoxicating as Captain Ransom the man. He drank in the man as if his thirst would never be quenched. Everything around him blurred away and there was only sensation and Ransom.

Their lips parted. Ransom's breathing was ragged. "Your kiss is more intoxicating than the strongest grog I've ever tasted. You are an amazing man, Clinton Porter." He tapped his glass to Clint's and they tossed them back. Refills arrived.

"I think your drink… or something… has gone to my head. I need to slow down. I haven't eaten yet." In spite of his statement he found himself taking a sip of his new drink. But he knew it was Captain Ransom St. James that had gone to his head… and everywhere else. The man was beyond sexy. "Could we go out on deck? I need some air."

"Of course. Are you feeling all right? Ransom grabbed his forearm.

Again that burning sensation. "I'm fine. More than fine. Great, in fact. That was a little effusive.

Ransom smiled. "After you," he said, opening the door to the deck.

The four, large, masted sails loomed above them. Clint looked up and felt overwhelmed as the sea breeze hit him. He fell backward a step. Ransom steadied him with a firm hand on his back. His drink sloshed onto his hand. He switched it into his other and raised the drink-soaked one to his mouth. He glanced up over his shoulder at Ransom, who still had a steadying hand on his lower back. Their eyes locked and Clint licked the stickiness from his fingers. Ransom's eyes darkened as Clint played into the sensuality of what he was doing, his tongue savoring the taste and the sensation. Ransom's lips parted while he watched the exhibition. Clint popped his thumb into his mouth and slowly withdrew it. Ransom voiced a sharp intake of breath, his hand squeezing harder on Clint's spine.

"I didn't want to waste any," Clint said diffidently, thinking that his own ardor mirrored Ransom's.

"Do you want help?" came the rejoinder.

"I think I got it all. But thank you for the offer." Whoa! He'd never done that before. He must be drunk to have done something so forward. "Oh wow, I'm so sorry. I've never done anything like that before. You must think I'm some kind of slut. That was decl—"

"Don't apologize. No need. And I don't think any such thing. I do think, however, that you are one of the most attractive men I've ever encountered. And if you do that again, I will not be held responsible for my actions." He spun Clint around to face him and leaned in close.

Clint could smell the sweet liquor on his breath and the tangy scent of the man. Ransom was going to kiss him. He closed his eyes.

"Understand?

The slight puff of liquory breath caused Clint to open his eyes. "Sorry, I... yes, I understand."

"Come, my laddie, let me show you my ship. He took Clint's hand and led him around on a tour of entire upper deck.

Clint observed other groups and pairs of men engaged in animated conversations; the excitement of the first day of the voyage was in the air. They quaffed their multi-colored drinks and plotted their upcoming conquests. It was a giant, floating, gay bar.

The realization struck him. He was soon done with this whole scene: the game playing, the role playing, the teasing, the awkward post-sex goodbyes, and on a ship it would be even more awkward. You'd see last night's hook-up for the next several days. He glanced at Ransom who had stopped to answer a question from a very beefy man in a three-sizes-too-small wife-beater. The guy was definitely hot, but way too obvious, and obviously very into himself. His name was probably Brick or Chance or Ridge.

Ransom turned to him. "Clint, this is Chance."

Bingo.

"He lives in Malibu."

Of course he does. "Nice to meet you, Chance." Clint nodded at the man.

"Dude, you're really frickin' hot too! You guys wanna hook-up later? I've got a great cabin and some really fun toys."

Ugh. And then he spoke. Not so hot anymore.

"Or, hey, I wouldn't mind just watchin' the two of you."

Whatever happened to class?

"Uh…" was all Clint could say.

"Thank you, Chance. We'll keep you in mind," Ransom said way more politely than Chance deserved. But Clint was sure it wasn't the first jerk he'd dealt with.

"Awesome! Can't wait!" And before Clint knew it, a ham-fist grabbed the back of his neck and his mouth was covered in a wet kiss. When Chance was done he grabbed Ransom and repeated the action. "Fuckin' sweet! Later, dudes. You know where to find me... the bar or the gym. He raised his arms and flexed his biceps. "For you, guys."

Clint noted that Chance did have big arms; it was just too bad his ego was even bigger, which probably meant something else wasn't. Which made him think about Ransom. *God! I'm as bad as Chance.* Then he wondered if Ransom was thinking the same thing about him. Talk about a whirlwind... He'd only been on the trip a few hours and he'd gotten drunk, flirted embarrassingly with the ship's captain, and been asked to have a threesome with a musclebound hunk whose IQ matched the size of his penis. What was next? A mud-wrestling orgy with hermaphroditic midgets? He needed to eat... and stop drinking. He took another sip, and looked at his glass—almost empty. *Shit.*

"Ahem." Charley.

"Thanks, Charley, but I need to slow down. Food. I need food."

"It's all right, Charley. Thank you," Ransom said, taking Clint's empty glass and handing it to the steward, along with his own. "Dinner should be ready. Shall we?" He indicated the direction with his arm.

"Later, right guys?" said the all-but-forgotten Chance.

Was he still here? Clint gave a glance at the gym rat and went through the door to the lower deck. Ransom smiled at Chance and followed.

Clint found himself walking along the corridor a little unsteadily, and he felt that warm familiar hand on his back again.

"I hope Captain Ransom wasn't your undoing?" The words were whispered softly into Clint's ear.

For a moment Clint tried to decipher what Ransom had just said. The drink. He was talking about the drink. Little did he know, it was Captain Ransom the man that might be his undoing. Was he falling for him already? He felt his life changing before his eyes. He was Ulysses caught between Scylla and Charybdis. Scylla was his old life: a nine-headed beast. Charybdis was… Ransom? a bottomless whirlpool that was swallowing him up. Was that a bad thing? He knew he wanted a life change. That he was certain of. And Chance-y the muscle-dude had just reinforced his feelings that that was the life he didn't want. Not anymore. He had been there, done that, and done that again. He was feeling disgusted with himself and his semi-sordid past. He'd thought he had more sense than that.

New chapter. New leaf. New life. Was it because of Ransom? No. It was his wake-up call. His final realization. There was more to life than superficiality and sex. Ransom appeared happy with his life. He'd found himself and what he enjoyed doing. What was his history? Clint would have to find out. He definitely wanted to know the man better.

What had Ransom just asked him? He turned around to him. "I'm sorry, I was woolgathering."

White teeth showed in a tanned face. "I asked if my drink was your undoing."

"No, not at all. I love it. I do need some food though."

"Our table awaits, me hearty." He leaned in close. "Aargh."

Clint laughed. "You do that very well. A lot of practice? You seem to have the style down."

A cloud briefly passed over the handsome visage and Clint thought he caught a glimpse of something... painful? Regretful? He couldn't quite discern it, but there was something.

"Aye, practice." Ransom's smile was a tad too bright. "Let's eat." He indicated the door behind Clint.

The meal was excellent and Ransom explained they had hired a Cordon Bleu chef for them. "Only the best for you. Every day will be a new menu, but if there is a particular dish you enjoy, Chef Ferenc will be happy to prepare it for you."

"I could get used to this, except I'd weigh three-hundred pounds in no time," Clint said, patting his lips with the red cloth napkin.

"I don't believe you would ever let yourself look less than perfect." Ransom raised his glass to his.

Clint recalled looking in the mirror before dinner and felt himself blush, but quickly responded, "Nor you." He clinked back.

"Dessert?"

"Remember what I said about three-hundred pounds? I'm going to pass, tonight anyway. And... I hope you don't mind, but I'd like to turn in early. I want to be well-rested for tomorrow. Isn't it a full-day stop in Grand Cayman? I hear it's beautiful and I'd like to take my time and explore, and I'd like to try scuba diving. I know they give a lesson beforehand. I've never done it and I've always wanted to. I'm sure you're an expert."

"Grand Cayman is beautiful, and if you don't mind, I would like to accompany you and show you a few places off the beaten path. I do know how to scuba dive and can help you with that as well."

"Oh, I didn't realize you could leave the ship."

"I'm the captain."

"Right." Clint nodded. "In that case, I wouldn't mind at all." This time Clint raised his glass to Ransom's.

"A stroll on the deck before you retire?"

"I think that would be the perfect way to end the night." Clint couldn't resist adding, "Almost perfect."

Ransom raised an eyebrow. "Almost."

They wandered to the deck and stood looking out at the moon's reflection off the dark Caribbean waters. Small waves lapped onto the side of the ship and the slow rocking motion was hypnotically tranquilizing. Ransom had his arm lightly around Clint's waist.

Clint breathed in the scent of him. Intoxicating.

"Do you have any idea how much I want to kiss you right now?" Ransom's light beard brushed the side of his cheek. His breath and words entered his ear.

"I think so," Clint responded, feeling the hard, lower part of his body pressed into his.

Ransom softly laughed. "Your decision."

Clint turned fully into him, their lips inches apart. "I'm not trying to tease you. That's not my style. But I would like to wait… I can't give you a logical, or even illogical, reason why. I just know I'm right."

"That's fine. I respect your decision. But…" Ransom pulled him in closer. "…if I see you with another man, I will not be responsible for my actions." He kissed Clint lightly on the forehead.

"Duly noted, and you needn't worry on that score. I hardly noticed there were other men on board." He looked solemnly into Ransom's eyes. "Except for the thirty or so half-naked, muscled, ripped guys with no underwear." He returned a light kiss to Ransom's forehead and pushed him away.

Ransom's eyes sparkled, even in the starlit night, and he laughed. "All right then, my handsome fellow. You may joke with me, but I am serious." He grabbed Clint's hand and brought it to his lips. Then with the lightest and most tender touch, kissed his palm. "And remember, I am the captain."

Clint felt the soft brush of lips on his skin down to his toes and a definite emphasis in his mid-section. How could that lightest of touches cause such an intense feeling? What would making love be like? And Clint was sure it would be making love and not just sex.

"Tomorrow?"

Clint gave him a puzzled look.

"Grand Cayman? Scuba diving?"

Clint shook his head to clear it.

"Perhaps you do need some rest. I will give you the Captain's Special Island Tour."

"Special?" Clint thought that anything with him would be special, as he recalled the plans for the tour they'd made a short while ago ago.

"Shipwrecks, rare and exotic animals, white sand beaches…" Ransom pulled Clint into him again.

Clint drew in a quick breath as their hips collided and he felt Ransom's still ardent desire. It seemed everything was special about the captain.

"I'm glad I learned to dive," Clint managed to say.

"As am I. I have been to the Cayman Islands many times over the years, on various ships."

Clint said, "How long have you been doing this?" wanting to keep their body contact as long as possible.

"More years than you'd think. There have been other vessels, not only the cruise ships." He looked off into sea above Clint's head.

Clint could see his thoughts went somewhere else and was about to pursue the subject—

"You should get a good night's rest." He released Clint and took a step back. Clint felt a pang of loss. "You will be surprised how tranquilizing the sea can be. You will sleep soundly but awaken with a new vigor. I am very sorry to say I will not be able to join you for breakfast. I have a few duties to attend to when we dock. I am sure that one or more of the—how did you put it?—half-naked-muscled-ripped guys… with no underwear would be happy to join you. However, I recommend a beautiful room-service breakfast on your private patio. I'll have Charley arrange it for you."

"And will Charley be joining me?"

"Alas, no. Charley also has port duties. Perhaps a good book?"

Ransom could not have been more disingenuous, and Clint loved it. Ransom had laid his claim and was not shy about it. "Well, I did promise myself that I would finally get through *Moby Dick*.

Ransom froze.

"You've read it? Clint said, questioning Ransom's reaction.

"I am familiar with it," Ransom said somewhat guardedly.

"Not a fan I take it. Still it is a classic… and as dry as it is, I promised myself I would barrel through it. I flipped through to some of the action scenes. They are very vivid. Herman Melville knows his subject matter well.

"Yes, he did," Ransom muttered, looking off again.

Clint noted the thousand-yard stare. He wanted to say something else, but it seemed inappropriate. He didn't know this man at all, and this seemed personal. "You know, now that I think about it, this trip is supposed to be fun so maybe I'll read the religious thriller instead. Escapism, right? Tomorrow then?" He was trying to bring back the light mood.

"What? Yes… yes tomorrow." He looked at Clint, focusing. "Goodnight, Clint."

"Goodnight, Ransom." What had changed? *Moby Dick*?

Maybe he'd look at it again.

And he did. Two hours' worth. He was hooked on Ahab and Ishmael. It had started slowly, but there was something about the realism of their story. He could almost smell the salty, cold Atlantic Ocean. But, of course, he was on a ship at sea so that may have accounted for the smell. But every detail of Ishmael's story put him right on board the Pequod. What was Ransom's aversion to it? For that's what Clint felt it was, something distressing or repugnant to it. There was a lot more going on with Captain Ransom St. James than met the eye. Although, what met the eye was incredible to behold. Well… as his favorite heroine said as he closed the book for the night, "Tomorrow is another day."

He closed his eyes and dreamed of a dashing pirate and a great white whale.

* * *

Knock. Knock. Knock. "Clint, Are you up yet? Breakfast." Charley.

Clint's eyes fluttered open, rousing him from the sexiest dream he'd ever had. He threw back the sheet.

Oops. Yes he was definitely up. And naked. Not much he owned was going to hide it. "Uh, Charley… could you just leave it outside the door?"

"It's kind of awkward to set down," came the voice from the other side of the door. "I'll close my eyes," he said, adding, "if you want." Clint heard him giggle.

Ah, what the hell... It is a gay cruise. He was sure Charley had seen it (and probably a lot more) before. And he wasn't particularly modest.

He opened the door, stepping back to let Charley through the narrow doorway.

Charley stared for a moment at Clint, dropped his eyes, smiled appreciatively, and walked in. "I'll set it out on your patio deck." He crossed to the partially opened sliding glass door, and with his foot, slid it open far enough for him and the tray to pass through. He set it down and came back into the room. "Anything else?" he said to Clint, who was still poised at the door.

Clint felt the heat rise in his face. Charley was cute... and he was still aroused. He shook his head. "No, that's fine. Thank you, Charley. I thought you had shore duties?"

"I do, but I thought I would personally drop off your breakfast first." Charley walked toward Clint, reached out a hand and squeezed. "The captain's a lucky man." He released Clint and went out the door.

The captain. Clint's thoughts returned to his vivid and very sexual dream. He needed to calm down. Coffee. That and some food should help. Then: first stop Grand Cayman Island.

He dug out some shorts from a drawer, grabbed *Moby Dick*, and went out to his patio. The Windjammer was docked—moored, he guessed was the correct term, and the small skiff?—tender?— would take them to shore. "God, I'm so bad at nautical jargon." He took a sip of coffee then pointed his index finger up. "Okay. The stern's the back. The prow... front, or is it the bow? Starboard, right. Port, left. Fore and aft, front and back. This is ridiculous. I'll ask the captain. It'll give us something to talk about." Then his thoughts turned to the captain's "stern," which was one of the best he'd ever seen. And from the way Ransom had filled out his slacks the previous evening, Clint was sure his "main mast" was impressive as well. These thoughts did little to lessen his own ardor, and he found himself stiffening again. Maybe he should have let Charley help him out after all. Food. That's what he needed... then a cold shower. He looked down at the table and remembered his book. He picked up the tome and looked at the cover. "This should get my mind focused. All right, Captain Ahab, let's see what you're going to do next." He opened the book, removed his bookmark that looked like a movie clapper, firmly planted his thumb in the middle to hold it open, and with his other hand, reached for a piece of toast, then settled in to read for the next few minutes before getting ready for the day's adventures.

"Good morning, me fine lads. This is your captain speaking." The speaker in his room roused Clint from Ishmael and Ahab. "Welcome to Grand Cayman Island! All of you wishing to explore the sights of this island paradise—and I highly recommend you do— the first tender will be leaving in fifteen minutes. We'll be arriving in the capital, Georgetown. So rouse yourselves from your rum-induced slumbers and make your way to deck three, mid-ship. Enjoy yourselves in beautiful Grand Cayman!"

Clint had jumped up at the start of the announcement and was in the shower before it ended.

Clint made his way to the lower deck. He assumed Ransom would be there.

And there he was. Again in white: white shorts, shoes, T-shirt—tight T-shirt. He'd shaved, and while there was still a little shadow-beard, the stubble was completely gone. Surfer-pirate: Ransom St. James. Hot as ever.

"You shaved. I like it," Clint said.

"I hoped you would. I like to look a little more clean-cut for shore excursions. Besides which, if I happen to steal a kiss, I don't want to leave whisker-burn as evidence."

Before Clint could recover from that aside with something bordering on intelligent, two young blond men, who had obviously "found each other" the night before, approached, and Ransom turned to them. "Good morning, gentlemen. Enjoy your day. The last tender departs from Georgetown at 4:45. Cocktails on board at 5:30."

The blonds smiled at Ransom and said together, "We'll be there." They laughed at their timing and strode down the ramp.

"Ready?" Ransom turned to Clint.

"That's it? No more? Don't you have to attend to the other passengers?" Clint was still thinking about stolen kisses and whisker-burn. Who cares about whisker-burn?

"Privileges of being captain. Charley will take over.

And from the bowels of the ship, Charley appeared, all smiles and energy. "Enjoy your day, Captain, Clint."

31

"We will. Thank you, Charley. After you, Clint."

Clint started down the ramp then heard Ransom say, "Those shorts fit you quite well." Clint felt his face and the back of his neck redden. "And you blush beautifully." Clint could feel the heat grow on his face and could feel Ransom's eyes locked on his backside as he followed.

For 9:00 A.M., the town and the beaches were quite crowded. Clint could see a large cruise ship moored out a little farther than theirs, probably causing the influx of people. Still, the town was quaint with a lot of white buildings.

"I thought we'd go the southern route of the island and eschew the town for now. It's quite crowded as you can see. Later, we can come back and sample the beers at the excellent local brewery, which I think you'll enjoy."

"Sounds great. A little early for beer anyway. I want a clear head for diving."

"Most definitely. We'll take a taxi to the Pirate's Caves first."

The drive was quick and Ransom informed Clint about some points of interest along the way.

Leaving the taxi, Ransom said, "In the 1700s, and even the 1800s, these caves were where pirates would hide their booty, as they say."

Clint listened while he admired the beautiful white sand beaches.

"Also, the beaches are so white and powdery soft because they are formed from the desiccated shells of the local marine life.

They stopped walking, and Ransom leaned into Clint's ear. Clint felt the heat emanating from the captain and inhaled his musky scent. "Which, as you will now experience, is also why the sand is not only white but powdery as well."

"I didn't know that," Clint managed.

"I know lots of things."

Clint felt the lightest brush of lips on his ear and nearly gasped aloud.

"Let's take off our shoes, and we'll walk the rest of the way to the caves enjoying the feeling of the lightest powder between our toes and on the soles of our feet."

Ransom's words brushed over Clint's ear like air-kisses. He would have removed all of his clothes right then if Ransom had asked.

They removed their shoes and made their way to the caves.

"We'll do the self-guided tour, if that suits you, and I'll show you a couple of my favorite labyrinthine areas in the caves."

"Sounds mysterious. Lead the way."

"The storm in 2004 opened up quite a few of the caves that were unknown prior to that," Ransom said, taking a sharp left in the dark cavern they'd just entered.

Clint's eyes were still adjusting to the stark contrast from the sun and white to the dank and dark of the caverns. The sound of the waves inside the caverns was intensified by confinement, and Clint felt as if the ocean was going to wash in and swallow them up.

"The area I'm taking you to I'm certain hasn't been seen in a hundred years or more. I don't even know if anyone besides myself has seen it."

"How did you know it was there? Isn't it dangerous to wander here by yourself?" Clint's foot slipped on a jutting piece of rock and he started to fall.

A firm hand grabbed him. "I've got you."

"Thanks. I didn't see it. I'm not clumsy normally. And my eyes still haven't adjusted."

"My dark eyes do adjust more easily. Please forgive me. I should have known better."

"It's nothing—"

"No! You could have been injured. I have been accused of being reckless in my day. You would think by now I would have learned." Ransom shook his head in disgust.

"Really, Ransom, it's not all your fault. I should have waited till my eyes were more adjusted. That was dumb."

"I brought you here and you are in my charge, therefore my responsibility. I will not allow it to happen again. You have my word."

Clint smiled now, enjoying for the first time since he could remember someone who genuinely cared about his safety. He liked it. "All right. You win this one, 'O Captain, my Captain.'"

"Whitman. You do realize he was writing about the death of Abraham Lincoln? But I appreciate the metaphor. You enjoy nineteenth-century literature then?"

"I guess you'd think so, what with *Moby Dick* and all." Clint tried to see Ransom's expression, and if he'd hit a nerve bringing up the book again, but it was too dark to make out anything there. "I really haven't read that much of it at all. Coincidence. You like to read?"

"Very much. I've read most of the classics many times."

"You have a favorite?"

"Jules Verne. His visions, which have proven to be true, always amazed me. It was fascinating to see his ideas become reality." Ransom paused and cleared his throat. "Of course, I enjoy the adventuring, and any of his novels that dealt with the sea."

Clint didn't respond immediately, taking in what Ransom had just said. "He would be my favorite too. I love adventuring, as you put it, and it makes me realize that maybe that's something that's been missing from my life. The only "adventuring" I've done the past few years is on a movie set. Total unreality and superficiality—like the people associated with it. What we're doing right now, going to pirate caves, seeing actual places where pirates stored their treasures… this is what's exciting!" And Clint realized he meant every word he said. He wanted real adventures. And Ransom could give that to him.

Ransom reached out and grabbed him, pulling him in close. The movement was so quick, if Ransom hadn't been holding him, he would have fallen on the rocks.

His mouth was covered by Ransom's.

Clint opened his mouth in immediate acceptance and Ransom's tongue captured his in a scorching kiss that made him weak-kneed. The water splashed around them. They clutched each other close. Clint felt the magic in the kiss and the man. This was what he was looking for. And if this was only from a kiss… he couldn't wait for more. He let himself get lost in the sensations, his mind void of anything but the moment and Ransom.

The kiss slowly broke and Ransom pulled back just enough to see Clint's eyes. His warm stammering breath assaulting Clint's lips, mingled with Clint's own stammering breaths. "You are the most amazing man I've ever met."

The whispered words made Clint's heart stop as he realized the words could have been his to Ransom, so he said them: "Yes, you are."

Ransom ransacked his mouth again in an even more scorching kiss than before. Clint was undone.

At last they stopped.

"This is not the most conducive location for this, and I can't believe we are both still standing on these slippery rocks," Ransom said, looking down at the precarious way they were standing, feet spread apart, straddling two large boulders. "I'm not sure who is holding up whom at this point. But perhaps we should move on to a safer area, for I promise you this is not the last kiss of the day."

Clint felt his groin clutch at the words and the prospect of more. "Then let's move on."

Ransom took his hand and they made their way deeper into the cavern.

They walked in silence for a while, each lost in his own

thoughts, Clint trusting Ransom to lead the way.

They took a sharp left and Ransom said, "Be careful here, the rocks are particularly precarious and I don't want you to get hurt, but I want to show you something that no one else has seen for hundreds of years."

Clint cocked his head in curiosity. "How do you know?"

"It's a secret." Ransom winked.

They stopped. There was a small cave entrance and the floor seemed quite dry.

"The storm I told you about a few years ago uncovered this. Come on." Ransom took Clint's hand.

They walked a couple of hundred feet inside. Then, immediately before them, a nook revealed itself containing a cache of small chests. "Are these what I think they are?" Clint said, staring in disbelief.

"If you mean treasure chests then, yes," Ransom said. "The men, pirates if you will, stored them all here. Granted, they are not the large chests you see in the movies, but each one has some kind of treasure, jewels, weapons, etc. Help yourself." He bent over and raised the lid of a nearby dark wood chest.

Clint sucked in a breath. "Oh my God, real pirate treasure!" He bent down and picked up a gold bracelet. "This is incredible. There must be a fortune here."

"I'm certain of it. But I have no need for it. I came upon it a couple of years ago in one of my cave explorations here. Would you care for some of my booty?" Ransom leered.

Clint got the implication but was too overawed to respond to it. "I couldn't. It's not mine."

"At this point and time, the owners are long dead. Maybe one piece then, as a souvenir?"

"I…" Clint stuttered then thought for a moment. "Why not? This is certainly a unique 'souvenir,' as you put it." He reached into the small trunk and withdrew a simple gold circlet that he thought would fit his wrist. He slid it on. "This'll do."

"Very nice, and simple. It suits you." Ransom gave Clint a quick peck on the lips.

Clint even felt that light brush of his traveling south. "This is amazing," he said. "Have you thought about telling someone, or taking it back as a discovery?"

"No, it doesn't interest me to do so. I enjoy knowing it's here. I will let some other adventurous type stumble upon it one day and do with it what he will. But I wanted you to see it. I thought you would appreciate it."

"Oh I do. And I like the fact, knowing it's here. It's kind of our secret." Clint bent his head, thinking, This is ridiculous. I feel like some inexperienced schoolgirl. He looked at his bracelet and spun it around his wrist.

"Our secret, yes." He tilted Clint's head up and planted a long sensual kiss on his lips. "There are so many secrets in life, my love." Their faces were inches apart. "That is life."

Clint noticed the odd look in his eyes but was too overcome by the words "my love" to think about it. This is going so fast. But it feels so right."

"Come." Ransom took Clint's hand. "I have more things to show you on this beautiful island. Please keep ahold of my hand so that there aren't any more accidents." He squeezed Clint's hand more firmly. "I also love the feeling of your warm hand in mine."

Clint's mouth dropped open slightly, as if to say something, but he couldn't think of any response.

"Next stop, the Botanic Gardens."

* * *

"These—what did you call them?—banana orchids are beautiful," Clint said, reaching out a hand to caress the flower.

Ransom closed his hand over Clint's and said, "They are very delicate. They are also the national flower. I'm glad you like them."

Clint breathed in Ransom, his smell more intoxicating than any flower, the warmth of the hand on his emphasizing the intimacy of the moment. "You are quite knowledgeable about the island. It's great to have my own private tour guide... especially one as handsome as you are."

Ransom pulled him close and stared into his eyes. "None of the beauty here can compare to the beauty of what I'm looking at right now."

Clint swallowed, feeling his eyes water. He had never heard anything so romantic. He wanted to swoon, but how romantic would that be? Instead, he leaned into Ransom and kissed him, letting him know how much those words had affected him. "Thank you," he whispered as their lips parted.

Ransom smiled warmly. "The blue iguanas next?"

Clint's mind was still unfocused. "Who?"

Now Ransom laughed. "The national treasure of the island, also a delicious drink. Would you like to try one?"

"The drink or the lizard?"

"Both. Come with me. There's a small bar not too far from here that serves them… the drink, not the lizard. Then we'll go see them in person."

* * *

"This is delicious!" Clint said after his first sip of the blue concoction.

"Yes, they are. But be careful and don't drink it too fast. There is quite a bit of alcohol sneakily hidden by the fruity flavor." Ransom seemed not to heed his own advice and took a large swallow through his straw. He noticed Clint's stare. "I'm more used to these than you are."

"Aye-aye, Captain," Clint said, giving a mock stern face before taking an equally long pull on his straw.

"You have been warned."

"Does that mean you won't protect me from the man-eating iguanas?"

"They are herbivores. And I doubt you need protection from

anything."

Clint didn't respond. His inner thoughts intruded. *And how to do I protect myself from my feelings for you?*

They walked and drank for a few minutes. "There are so many butterflies here. It's really a paradise," Clint said, leaning in close to an especially brilliantly colored butterfly idly perched on a flower.

"I'm not sure of how many species are here, but there are many, that I do know. I'll have to find out."

"I'm glad you don't know everything. And now I have to admit that you were right about the drink… I'm starting to feel it."

"I won't say I told you so, but remember we have diving later on."

"How much later?"

"After lunch?"

"Food would be good. That'll do it."

"After we see the iguanas, I know a wonderful little grill that has a delicious fish fry and…" Ransom's hand shot out and he stopped Clint in his tracks.

"What—"

"Shh. To your right on that tree branch, just above the ground."

Clint turned his head and there it was: a blue iguana. It was sitting on the limb, sunning itself apparently; its eyes—at least the right one—stared at them.

"Your first blue iguana."

"They are blue," Clint said. "It's beautiful."

"One of my favorite of nature's creations. And incredibly docile."

"Amazing. Thank you."

"I had nothing to do with it. But I'm glad I could let you experience them."

"Are there more?"

"Many. The island has made sure that these creatures are protected and more than a thousand now exist, whereas many years ago they were near extinction. Now, on to the habitat and then the next part of our adventure."

"Lead the way, my Captain."

"Yes, your Captain."

Clint wasn't sure what Ransom meant exactly by his statement… but he liked it.

After the blue iguana habitat, they headed to Ten Sails Drive, and Ransom filled Clint in on more history of the island.

"These six blocks represent the six victims from the wrecks of the ten downed ships that sank there on the reef in 1794," Ransom pointed out to the reef, which was visible through the crystalline water.

They were alone on the windy promontory and Clint looked at the masculine profile, picturing the virile man commanding a ship—perhaps a pirate ship—in the 1800s. He sighed in admiration.

Ransom, apparently thinking the sigh was from the death of the sailors continued, "Yes, it was tragic, to think that all ten ships met their fate here. But it was early in the morning and communication was not what it is today. The fortunate thing that happened was that the townsfolk heard the distress calls from the ships and paddled out on canoes and ended up saving four hundred and fifty men. So you see, the tragedy could have been much, much worse."

"You really do know your history. It's fascinating, and you recount it so well."

"Thank you. I hoped I wouldn't bore you."

"I don't think you could ever do that." Clint clamped his mouth shut, fearing that might have crossed a line.

Ransom looked at him warmly and leaned in for a quick kiss.

The spark from that kiss caused Clint's arms to go up around Ransom's shoulders and he deepened the kiss.

Ransom finally pulled back slightly and said, "There's more."

Clint knew his own eyes darkened with anticipation.

"To the story," Ransom smiled and pulled back. "If you want to hear it that is. If we continue to kiss like that, I fear our entire excursion will be cut short—while that would be my first choice—I do not want to short shrift your experience."

That is exactly what I want, Clint wanted to say, but chose discretion this time. "I would like to have the full experience, Captain."

"Very well then." He gave Clint a quick peck on the nose. "There is a legend that says that when King George III heard of the bravery of the Caymanians, he rewarded them by decreeing that the

Cayman Islands would henceforth be free from taxation and war conscription."

"Well, that would explain the unique financial status here."

"Something which I am grateful for."

Clint gave a puzzled look.

"Where do you think I keep my own booty?" Ransom laughed.

A slow lascivious smile appeared on Clint's face.

Ransom laughed. "Not that booty, sexy boy."

Clint laughed as well. "So, you have secret offshore accounts, eh? Handsome and rich? You're quite the catch. I think you must have something hidden in your dark past."

Ransom's face darkened. There was an awkward moment. "There are some things…"

Clint smiled tentatively. "Well, who doesn't have a couple of things in their pasts."

"Like?" Ransom raised an eyebrow.

"I'll share mine, if you do."

Ransom stared deeply into his eyes. "Maybe you are the one. But now is not the time. Scuba diving awaits us."

The mood back to normal, Clint said, "Yes, I am anxious to see the shipwrecks from underwater."

"And I am anxious to show them to you. There is one especial ship that is seldom explored and not part of the regular tourist dives."

"Lead on."

* * *

The diving was spectacular. The water, warm and crystal clear. The local marine life, beyond anything Clint could have imagined.

They both wore the short silkies that had recently become popular, with their vests and tanks.

Clint admired the long powerful legs in front of him as Ransom made his way through the water, the silkies emphasizing his tight rear end.

Ransom, seemingly sensing the leer, turned back to Clint. He reached out a hand, which Clint took, and they proceeded through the water this way for a short time, until Clint started to make out the outline of a large wreckage.

They swam around the hull of the ship, along the side and to the stern. Ransom stopped there and pointed. Clint couldn't see anything at first, then he made out a hole in the far end of the deck about twenty feet away. They swam toward it. It was small, and a man could probably swim through it—which Ransom did.

Clint, surprised, held back. A hand shot out back through the hole. He once again took it and followed Ransom into the darkness.

A light appeared, illuminating the hold they'd just swum into. Ransom had brought a flashlight—a powerful one—and Clint was trying to figure out where he could have kept it, when they abruptly stopped. Ransom reached out to a pile of rotted wooden planks and pulled them back. He shined the light directly ahead and onto a large wooden chest.

Clint waited.

Ransom gestured for him to open it.

Clint's anticipation made him draw more swiftly on his regulator. He reached for the rusty hasp on the front and pushed up. Ransom reached for the side and helped him lift the lid.

Treasure.

The trunk was filled with all manner of gold and silver pieces, as well as numerous items of jewelry. Clint stared in awe. This was truly a king's ransom. His Ransom's. Who was this man? How had he found this? Why was it still here? More and more questions roiled through his head, the last being: Why has he shown me this? And the other treasure as well? A hand grabbed his forearm and Ransom pulled him in close. Ransom reached up and pulled out his regulator, then he reached for Clint's own and removed it.

Momentary panic seized Clint until he found his lips covered by Ransom's. Their mouths opened and their tongues connected. Clint forgot all of his questions and became lost in the peculiar and erotic sensations of his first underwater kiss. Breathing forgotten, all his attention focused on the mouth and body pressed to his, the silkies revealing Ransom's arousal matching his own.

Ransom pulled back and replaced the regulator in Clint's mouth before replacing his own. Their bodies still locked together, Ransom and Clint's eyes also locked together through their masks. They held this way for a few moments, then Ransom reached down and brought up a small gold band. He slipped it on Clint's finger. It fit perfectly. Clint noticed the significance of it on the ring finger of his left hand. I do, he thought.

Ransom reached down once again and closed the chest. He moved to the planks and covered up the hoard. Taking Clint's hand, they swam out of the hold and back into the open water.

They spent a while longer exploring and observing before resurfacing. They climbed back on board the small boat and removed their gear.

"That was the most incredible thing I've ever done. And more treasure! I don't know how you do it, but, thank you," Clint said to the near-naked Ransom, clad in silkies and nothing else.

"Thank you," Ransom said, looking meaningfully at him.

Pinter's plays should have so much subtext, Clint thought. "And now?" he said.

"The dock, a drive along the north part of the island, and a drink or two at the local brewery I told you about earlier." He reached for Clint's left hand. "It suits you. I hope you like it. I've never given anyone a ring before."

Clint's throat closed up and he couldn't respond. He simply nodded.

Ransom squeezed Clint's hand in response.

* * *

The local beer was excellent, as Ransom had promised.

"I like to end my day here watching the spectacular sunset."

Ransom finished his beer and signaled the waitress for another. "I am usually alone, and this particular sunset has been made all the more spectacular by my handsome company." He toasted Clint.

"I am not as eloquent, so I'll merely say 'ditto.'"

They stared off the bar's deck at the amazing conflagration of colors in the early evening sky.

As if reading Clint's thoughts, Ransom said, "I know you want to know more about me. There is much to tell and I fear you might not be, shall I say, receptive to it. It frightens me. In a brief period, I have grown very fond of you. I feel destiny has stepped in here, and for whatever reason—one that I will have to explain at a later time—I am going to pursue it. I hope that is all right with you. I sense your feelings are similar. This voyage is all too brief and I want to spend as much of it as I can with you."

Clint took long drink from his mug, as much to contain his feelings as to collect his thoughts. "You're dead on with your assessment. For whatever reason, fate has thrown us together, I'm along for the ride. I do want to know more about you. I want to know everything about you. I want you to know you can trust me. I know that perhaps I might be dipping into the unexplainable with you. I hate to say supernatural, but I think that's what it might be. I want you to know I'm prepared for that. Just tell me. My heart and my head are prepared." Clint stared hard at him, trying to make him believe what he was about to say. "My feelings are 'supernatural.' There's a spell or enchantment, or something, at work here. There is no logical explanation for any of this. So give me the illogical. If you don't tell me everything, then there's no chance for us." He choked up. "And more than anything, I want there to be a chance for us."

Clint's tears were reflected in Ransom's eyes. He spoke, "Clint, thank you. I believe you. I will explain as best I can the extraordinary circumstances that are my life. I promise that when we get to Haiti, I will tell you everything."

"Fair enough." He paused. "Can I ask you one question, and do you promise to answer truthfully?"

"Yes."

"When we get back to the ship, will you make love with me?"

Ransom's eyes darkened. "That is a certainty."

* * *

Ransom opened the door to his cabin. I would carry you in, but ships' doors are not accommodating to such romantic gestures.

Clint pictured himself being carried in Ransom's arms and felt a rush of heat. "It's definitely a design flaw."

Ransom closed the door, and with one quick movement, had Clint up against it and Ransom's mouth was devouring his mouth.

Clint's mouth readily opened to receive his tongue, and his arms enclosed the broad back.

"You are the most attractive man I've ever met," Ransom whispered in his ear. "I want to devour you." Proving it, he gave Clint's earlobe a small nip. Clint groaned.

Ransom took a step back and shucked his shirt; Clint

matched him and removed his as well. The dark eyes smoldered. "Magnificent."

"Sexy as hell," Clint countered.

"I believe that for the first time in my life, I'm trembling." Ransom raised his, indeed trembling, hand and stroked Clint's chest. "God has blessed you, my love."

Clint couldn't respond, or even move. That powerful hand was searing his flesh everywhere it brushed. He flinched when fingers brushed his hardened nipple, one of his most sensitive areas. "I am sensitive there as well." Ransom flicked the nipple again and gave the pectoral muscle a hard squeeze. Clint moaned louder and felt his knees buckle a little.

"Can we lie down, because if you do that again, I'm going to fall down."

Ransom chuckled. "What a perfect suggestion. I can't believe I didn't think of it." He reached up and tugged on both of Clint's nipples and drew him to him. "Follow me."

"Anywhere," Clint grunted and let himself be led to the king-sized bed.

"Don't move." Ransom locked eyes with Clint and slowly unzipped his shots, revealing himself fully. Clint stared, sure that every drop of saliva had just evaporated in his mouth. "Do I pass muster?"

Clint swallowed hard then said huskily, "I can't imagine a muster you wouldn't pass. God, you're perfect." He lowered his gaze. "Everywhere."

Ransom flexed his "everywhere" for Clint. "Now for my enjoyment, will you return the favor?

Clint suddenly felt shy. He reached for his fly and hesitated. How can I compare to this walking god of manhood?

"Please, Clint, you're torturing me. I've never desired any man this much. I have to have your body on mine. I'm aching. Please."

This final plea undid Clint. He wants me as much as I want him. He knew his pants weren't leaving much to the imagination at this point, especially with no underwear on under thin material. He slowly undid his pants.

"Yes," came the whisper, from the man who stood in front of him, almost frozen, totally enrapt.

Clint sprang free and Ransom drew in a sharp breath. He dropped his pants and kicked them away, standing brazenly on display for Ransom to gaze on.

"This is the moment and the man I did not believe existed. I could stare at you forever."

"The feeling's mutual, my captain, but I do want a little more," he ended wryly.

Neither knew who moved first, but in an instant they were one. Mouths, lips, tongues, hands were everywhere. They fell to the bed and… explored. Groaning, grunting, gasping. Neither could get enough of the other.

Every touch, every smell, every taste was Ransom. And they were all delicious. "Ransom, I want you to take me. Make us one."

"Whatever, you wish, my love. I will never deny you anything." He pulled Clint even closer and fulfilled his request.

Clint was no longer aware of anything but pure pleasure. He was lost in body… and heart. This was what his life had led him to: this man.

In moments, or hours later, he felt the most exquisite feeling he had ever experienced.

They lay in each other's each arms. Ransom spoke, "I have never experienced anything more incredible. Who are you Clinton Porter? All my life—"

Clint raised a finger to Ransom's lips then replaced it with his own lips, silencing any more conversation for the next hour.

* * *

A soft knock on the door woke the two men.

"Come in, Charley," Ransom said.

Charley entered the cabin with a cheery "Good morning" and a cart with several plates with silver covers.

"I knew you two would need to, uh, fortify yourselves after last night's merry-making. And we have docked at Cozumel. Your transportation to Tulum is ready when you are. So you may take your time. Enjoy the pancakes and Eggs Benedict. And each other. If you need me for anything, Captain, you know how to reach me. Have fun, gentlemen." Charley gave a wink to Clint and left.

"I think Charley likes you," Ransom said.

"Yes, he made that clear yesterday."

"Well, if there was this much of you on display, it's no wonder."

"What…" Clint glanced down and realized the only thing covering him was Ransom's arm around his shoulders, and a leg strategically placed between his legs. "Uh, there was. He caught me coming out of the shower."

Ransom's arm tightened around him. "And?"

"Nothing happened." He kissed Ransom's stubbly chin. "But he did offer."

Ransom relaxed his arm a little. "He has excellent taste, and I would be surprised that anyone wouldn't want to be with you."

"Well, Captain, obviously the right anyone hasn't shown up yet."

"Fools. And now?"

Clint looked up into warm, dark, questioning eyes. Was Ransom the right anyone? He wanted him to be. More than living. Living was Ransom. He'd made Clint come alive. He didn't know what to answer. Instead, he answered with a kiss, containing all the love he felt, hoping that Ransom would accept it as his response.

Ransom responded in kind and they enjoyed themselves for the next few minutes, as their eggs congealed and their pancakes cooled.

"Tulum?" Clint said, sliding on a pair of Ransom's shorts and a pale-green T-shirt. "And thank you for the clothes. It saved me a trip back to my cabin."

"I can have Charley move your things in here, if you so desire."

The look on Ransom's face of hope and expectation surprised Clint. This man really cares about me. "I would like that. If you're sure," he quickly added.

"I've never been more so. And my cabin is certainly large enough for the two of us."

"That's true. This must be the largest room—uh, cabin—on the ship."

"It is. And to answer your first question, yes, Tulum, the ancient ruins. I thought you would enjoy it, and it is one of my favorite sites in the Yucatán."

"With secret places?" Clint ventured.

"There might be one or two." He smiled and gave Clint a short but powerful kiss that left him wanting to just stay in the cabin all day.

"You and your secrets. You're the tour guide.." He opened the door for Ransom and they set off for ancient Tulum.

* * *

"This is breathtaking," Clint said as he stood at the top of the hill, the stone ruins before them and the crystal blue Gulf behind it."

"I am glad you think so. As did the Mayans. Not only was it the perfect place to defend invaders from the sea, it also provided an aesthetically pleasing vista for them." Ransom pointed off to the right. "Down over there is a roped-off area. Roped off for the tourists. Some of the structures have become unsound over the centuries—it has been eight hundred years—and the locals don't want any tourists tripping or falling on the rough rocks."

"I'm assuming roped off for tourists doesn't apply to you?"

"You're learning, my love. Blond, handsome, and intelligent." He took Clint's hand and led him down the hill to the ruins.

There were quite a few people in the area. A couple were obvious tour groups with their respective guides, others wandered by themselves.

"I assume you know all about this place, right?"

"Smarter and smarter… I do in fact know more than most."

"Please tell me."

"Very well, information first, secrets after."

"Yes, secrets." He squeezed Ransom's hand.

They stopped in a grassy area in front of a large edifice.

"This is the Castillo pyramid. It was the watchtower to observe any invaders from the sea. The Mayans started construction in the 1200s and it was in use until the late 1500s when our friends the Spaniards managed to bring disease to the 1500 or so people living here. Thereafter, it was abandoned. It was called Zama, city of dawn, as it faces the east and the rising of the sun. Each of the walls ran some 1300 feet in length, being ten to sixteen feet high and some twenty-six feet thick. Fairly impenetrable, I'd say."

"I'd say."

They walked a bit and stopped again. "This building is the

Temple of the Descending God, closed to the public, but it has a mural displayed that can be seen from the exterior. However if you wish to go inside…"

"Perhaps after the tour, Captain." Clint pointed of in the distance. "What about that building—ruin—out there?"

"Ah, anxious, are we? That building and the one on the opposite end are the Temple of the Wind and the Temple of the Sun, used in spiritual practices and astrological findings. The Mayans were strong believers in the stars, moon, sun, etc., and what they could tell and foretell as well. Which leads us to the secret place." He took Clint's hand and they walked toward the far building. "Do you believe in astrology or the spiritual, Clint?"

For some reason Clint thought this might be an important question. "I have never felt strongly one way or the other, until recently. I think there are forces and unknown powers that influence or guide, like this trip for instance. You for another."

"Me?"

"Yes, you, Captain Ransom St. James. You know none of this makes any rational sense. You're the ultimate man of mystery… yet I find myself trusting you. Some power or being is influencing this all. And I'm okay with it. I've always trusted my instincts and they have served me well. My gut tells me this is right and I'm right where I should be at this moment in time. With you."

They had stopped in front of the medium-sized ruin.

Ransom stared at him warmly, but seriously. "You are right in everything you say. There are forces at work here, beyond our comprehension. I am a man of mystery, as you put it. You are right to trust me and your instinct. I am trusting my own as well. It has gone too far too quickly with us. This has never happened to me. You are the supernatural one. You make me feel things I didn't think were possible for me anymore. And I still may be wrong. But if you are willing to risk this with me, whatever the ultimate outcome, then so be it. Are you, Clint? Are you willing to risk it all? All on some broken-down, scruffy, bum of captain of a gay cruise ship?"

Ransom's self-deprecation made Clint laugh out loud. "You could never be any of those things. But to answer your question, most emphatically yes. I will risk it all. I have already felt things I never have, and no matter the outcome, as you so ominously put it, I wouldn't give up those feelings for anything. If, God forbid, I never saw you again, I would still be happy. You know the old bromide: 'It's better to have loved and lost—'"

"'than never to have loved at all.' Lord Tennyson, a personal favorite."

"Wow, you never cease to surprise me. I knew the quote but not the poet."

"Come." Ransom pulled him hard and they stepped around a roped-off barrier and entered the building. The temperature dropped a good fifteen degrees from their being out in the sun.

Ransom stopped and pulled Clint close. "Do you love me?" Ransom's eyes had filled with emotion.

Clint hesitated. Do I? Don't lie to yourself. Of course you do! "I've never felt anything so strong or powerful or felt so deeply. I'm scared, a little, but I can't deny it. I do love you."

Ransom pulled him close and covered his mouth in a soul-searing kiss. "Oh, my love, that is what I want, need, yet... I am so afraid... afraid I will lose you, as I have lost everything else."

His next kiss held an intensity and desperation that almost frightened Clint, but that didn't stop him from returning the kiss with all the intensity and passion it demanded.

They broke apart, both breathless and burning for one another. Silently, Ransom led Clint into the building. Before them lay small stone slab.

"I have had this fantasy all day. This is the chamber of the Temple of the Sun where rites, and, I have heard, sacrifices were performed to the gods." He looked at Clint in the cool, dimly lit space. "Will you be my sacrifice?"

Clint felt himself being aroused. Sacrifice? "Yes, my amazing love, take me."

It began with kissing, then fondling, then the discarding of clothes. The room was cool; their bodies were hot. They were both naked, yet sweat formed on their backs and chests, making their hands slick as they frantically explored each other, as if for the first time, both knowing there really was no turning back for either of them.

Ransom slid an arm under Clint and picked him up, gently settling him on the stone slab. Clint cried out as the cold from the stone shocked his heat-stricken backside. Ransom climbed up and stood over the recumbent Clint. Proud. Magnificent. Hard muscles glistening sweat in the dim light. Ready to be the conquering hero and take his prize.

Clint's breathing was ragged. Raw desire filled him. He needed this man.

Ransom came down on him, his body burning his front, while his back received the cold from the stone. The sensation was indescribable and driving him crazy. "Take me." It was a near yell.

Ransom entered him and he nearly passed out from the incredible feeling. Clint clutched and pulled at him, desperate for more of the man. He was a wild beast, rutting, striving for his goal.

It came for both of them in a near blinding flash of bliss, both screaming out each other's names, their cries echoing in the empty chamber.

The sacrifice had been made. Hopefully, the gods were appeased. They both were.

They stayed locked together for some time, their sweat-slicked bodies still glued together. Neither wanted to move or for the moment to end. "Can we die now? I don't want this to end," Clint said into Ransom's sweaty neck.

"Nor do I, my love. But there is more."

"More? I don't think I can do this again. I know it would kill me this time." He gave an involuntary shiver as his sweat began to dry in the cool chamber.

"You are cold?"

"Not with your hot body on top of mine. I'm surprised we didn't melt the slab. Do you think the gods appreciated our sacrifice?"

Ransom laughed and his chest bounced on Clint's. "I am not sure... but I am sure they never had a sacrifice quite like this one."

Clint laughed back, but not quite as deeply, as he was still underneath Ransom, who now wiggled his hips a bit.

Clint could feel him still hard inside him. "Is this slab some kind of magical Viagra?"

Ransom kissed him deeply. "The slab does not have the magic... you do."

Those words brought Clint back into the game, and they began again. If there was déjà vu, this was it for the two men. In a complete reenactment of the previous minutes, they found themselves both, ultimately, screaming each other's names as they rode the waves of ecstasy.

Walking from the Temple, Clint, still bathing in the afterglow of insanity, said, "Maybe we should make a sacrifice in the other temple, the Temple of the Wind?"

"In a heartbeat, my love, but as you can see, the sun will be setting soon. And while I long to stay for as long as you'd like, I have a ship to set sail and others depend on me to see to it."

"Next time?" Clint hoped he'd kept the desperate hope out of his voice.

Ransom tried to hide his hint of melancholy, saying, "Next time we'll sacrifice in all of the buildings, my love."

"Promise?"

"It is my most fervent wish."

Clint could see that he meant it, and he smiled. "Do we have plans tomorrow?"

"Yes."

"Are you going to tell me?"

Ransom grinned brilliantly, melancholy gone. "Why would I do that?"

"Does it involve lovemaking?"

"Of that, you can be sure."

"Then the rest doesn't matter. One more thing."

"Yes?" They stopped walking.

"I love you."

Ransom's eyes filled and Clint saw him swallow hard. He kissed Clint tenderly on the lips. "I love you, my dearest Clint."

Clint felt his own eyes fill. And he nodded.

* * *

The next day was an "at sea" day, so Clint learned the terminology. "At sea" meant they didn't dock anywhere, so there were multiple activities on board.

Clint lay with his head on the chest of his sound asleep captain, thoroughly engrossed in the tale of the white whale.

He heard a grumble. "Are you still reading that damn book?"

"Yes, I like it. Ahab is like you in many ways."

Clint felt Ransom's body stiffen and his chest flex. "You think so?"

"Yes, eerily so. He's arrogant, brash, a take-charge type of guy—"

Ransom sat up abruptly, dislodging Clint and his book. "I lost my page—"

"Is that how you see me?" It was almost a shout.

Clint was taken aback. He lowered his voice. "No, Ransom. I was kidding. Yes, you are commanding and know how to take charge. I've seen how you run the ship and the respect you get. They all love you... including me. You're gentle, kind, considerate, generous, loving—now I'm making you sound like a Boy Scout. I mean, you're... well, I guess you're really not much like Ahab at all. I don't know why I said you were. Maybe because he was a ship's captain... I don't know. I'm sorry. I'm blond. Forgive me?"

Ransom stared at him then pulled him into his arms. "There's nothing to forgive, my love. I am a fool. A fool who wants to be everything to you. I over-reacted to the comparison." He kissed the top of Clint's head. "Ahab was an ass. A braggart. A blowhard. A pompous—"

Clint pulled back and silenced him with a kiss. "I get the idea. You don't like him. He's not very likeable. I feel sorry for poor Ishmael, though. He puts up with him. I mean, I know how it all ends. I've seen the movie—like, ten times. But the story has never been so vivid for me. I'm on the ship... with a hot ship's captain... I don't know. But it makes the book seem... romantic in a way. No. That's crazy. But somehow, it's not." He rubbed Ransom's hard pectorals. "Maybe I'm just an incurable romantic. Or maybe I want to be one. I want a happy ending. I want this to be my happy ending." He lightly punched a pec.

Ransom grabbed his fist. "I want this to be our happy ending too. More than you could ever know. There are circumstances… beyond my control… that… I promise I will tell you about when we get to Labadee tomorrow. There is someone there, a woman… a priestess. She has been trying to help me for many years. Perhaps, now that I've found you, things can be different. Will you trust me?"

The pain in his eyes touched Clint to his core. I'm totally lost, but I trust you." Then he added, "I have to." He picked up his book. "I don't need to finish this—"

Ransom grabbed his hand. "No. I want you to. It may help you to understand better."

Clint opened his mouth to speak, then shut it. "All right, Ransom. I only have a quarter of it to go."

"I have an idea. Why don't we lie here together. You may return to your spot on my chest—because I enjoy it. And why don't you let me read that other book you have—*The Third Hour*, I believe you said it was called? I'll have Charley bring us breakfast in bed. We will make love then explore the day's activities on board. There are some I am sure you will enjoy."

"Can I change the order a little?"

"Whatever you desire?"

"Well, I desire… you and the lovemaking first. Moby can wait."

"If that is your decision…"

63

* * *

"The ending is still sad," Clint said, making their way to "Drag Bingo" in the small theater on the ship's mid-level deck.

"It is a tragedy, I agree," Ransom said.

"All those men killed, except Ishmael, of course, but his life is ruined too. How do you get over something like that? And all because of one egomaniac's obsession." Clint stopped on the landing, heading down to the lower level and started to speak some more.

"On another note, I truly enjoyed *The Third Hour.* Very suspenseful and intriguing."

"Way to change the subject. I know you have some aversion to Moby—"

Two burly men dressed in Village People attire rushed by, cutting off Clint's comment. "Sorry, Captain, we want to get a good seat."

"So this 'Drag Bingo' is like regular bingo with a drag queen hosting and calling the numbers?"

"Yes…"

"I thought the Line Dancing class was fun. You were really good. I liked the two-stepping the best."

"If I was good, it's because I had a great partner."

Clint smiled with pleasure at the compliment. "But I guess this Bingo is the hot ticket tonight?" Clint said after the men had passed. "And what were those outfits?"

"Actually, no. The hot ticket is the Captain's Reach-Around Disco Ball, hence the Village People outfits."

"I see. We're going?"

"I am the host. I think you'll enjoy it. And we don't have to stay all night. We may leave if you have something you'd rather do."

Ransom's implication was obvious and Clint instantly felt the rush of heat in his body. Playing coy, he said, "If you dress like the Construction Worker, I might be persuaded to leave early."

"I have my hard hat, suspenders, and holey jeans waiting to wear. I'll enjoy you removing them even more."

Clint's temperature rose even more at the thought, and not thinking if there was anyone around, pulled Ransom in for a tongue-blistering kiss, leaving no doubt the effect Ransom's fantasy had on him.

He ended the kiss, seeing the smoldering look in the dark eyes. "Maybe I'll leave on your boots and hard hat."

Ransom's eyes darkened even more.

Clint grabbed his hand and said, "Let's play Drag Bingo."

They walked into the theater and at the entrance was a beautiful "woman" in a red-hot, floor-length, blue-sequined gown.

"Good evening, gentlemen," he said.

Clint looked closely. "Charley?"

"In the flesh." He gave a slight curtsy.

"You look amazing!" Clint said.

"You look pretty hot yourself, sweetie," Charley said, and squeezed Clint's chest. "And you may call me, Goldie Booty, for tonight."

Ransom gently removed Charley/Goldie's hand from Clint's chest, where he was still fondling. "Goldie is our Bingo caller."

"Yes, I'll be handling the balls." Charley reached out a hand toward Clint's crotch.

Ransom slapped his hand away before Charley made contact. "Any balls but these." He furrowed his brow, causing Charley to step back and teeter on his heels. "They're spoken for."

Recovering, Charley said, "Aye, aye, Captain." He mock saluted. "There are other fish in the sea." He turned to leave then said over his shoulder, "But you definitely got the Catch of the Day."

Both men laughed at the departing Goldie.

"He's outrageous," Clint said.

"Yes... sometimes too much. I apologize for stepping in like that. But I got a sudden rush of jealousy. I shouldn't have spoken for you. Charley is very attractive and perhaps you—"

"What?" Clint sputtered. "Are you nuts? No pun intended. I have you! You're all I want." And once again, not caring who was around, he ground his mouth onto Ransom's. He pulled back an inch, "Or ever will want." He kissed Ransom again.

Applause broke their embrace, and Clint came back to reality. "I'm sorry, Ransom. You make me do crazy things I've never done. I'm sorry I embarrassed you."

"My love, you make me proud, not embarrassed. Every man in this room wishes your lips were locked on theirs. And this is a gay cruise after all. And, since I am the captain, I make the rules. I will kiss in public whomever I choose, and the devil with them if they don't like it. Now, let's find seats, Charley appears to be ready."

Clint sighed inwardly, not believing how lucky he was to find this man…

…or how lucky he was an hour later when Charley/Goldie shouted, "O-69," and Clint yelled, "Bingo," and won the coverall for one thousand dollars!

"Wow, I can't believe my luck!" Clint yelled, slightly out of breath.

"I cannot believe my luck either," Ransom said, and smothered Clint's mouth in a searing kiss.

Which prompted uproarious applause from the entire room.

They collected Clint's winnings and the congratulations from the men around them.

"Ready for my ball?" Ransom said, putting his arm around Clint.

"I don't have anything to wear."

"Perfect."

* * *

Later, in their cabin, Clint basked in the afterglow of what was once again incredible lovemaking. He lay in Ransom's arms breathing in his scent. "This has to be the best night of my life. I had no idea the party would be so fantastic. I've never danced like that… or so much. How did you learn all those crazy disco moves?" He rose up on one elbow to stare at the man who had changed his life. He reached up to adjust the hard hat Ransom still wore. "And I love your hard hat."

"Is that the only hard part you love, my love?"

Clint slid his hand down Ransom's naked body. Stopped and squeezed. "Hardly."

Ransom grunted in response. "Before you continue admiring my hard attributes, and I lose all reasonable thought, let me remind you that we dock at 8:00 in Labadee."

"I remember, Captain." He slid down Ransom's body. "Where all will be revealed."

Clint felt a momentary pang of fear. Then stopped his thoughts, reminding himself that he would only enjoy tonight and that everything would work out all right.

It had to.

* * *

Clint came awake to the sound of Ransom's voice coming over the speaker.

"Welcome to Haiti, everyone. It is a perfect day to see this enchanting island. It's sunny and the temperature is a tropical eighty-five degrees. Be sure to take your sunscreen; you won't want to burn anything you may need later on this evening. Debarking is mid-ship deck three. Enjoy yourselves in beautiful Labadee, Haiti."

The announcement made Clint smile. He had not even heard

Ransom leave earlier.

He cleaned up and dressed and made his way to the lower deck, where he assumed Ransom would be waiting, performing his requisite debarking "Welcome to Labadee. Be back by 5:00" speech.

And there he was, again in white: white shorts white shoes, white T-shirt—tight, white T-shirt. He'd shaved, and while there was still a shadow-beard, the stubble from the night before was completely gone. Surfer-pirate Ransom St. James: hot as ever.

He reached up to stroke Ransom's cheek. "Nice and smooth, just the way I like it."

"The stubble didn't seem to bother you last night."

"That was different. And most of the whisker-burn is hidden, and only a little tender."

He touched Clint's face. "I am glad that you have recovered. I will try to avoid the more sensitive areas next time, but I cannot promise."

Clint was about to say something risqué, when the same two young, blond men from the other day approached. Obviously things were working out for them.

A bright smile from Ransom. "Good morning, gentlemen. The last tender is at 4:45; cocktails at 5:30. Enjoy Labadee."

The two men smiled back, turned to each other, then said, "We'll be there."

"Well that was deja vu I'd say." Clint shook his head.

"You see, people can find one another on cruise ships. It's all not casual hook-ups. Ready?" Ransom looked at Clint.

"Of course."

"Ahoy, gemtlemen." Charley appeared, all smiles and energy, sans the high heels and false eyelashes. "Enjoy your day."

"We will. Thank you."

Clint jumped in, "Oh, thanks, Charley for pulling the winning ball last night at Bingo."

"O-69. How could you lose?" Charley laughed. "You're welcome, Clint. Have fun!"

"You walk first this time," Clint said. "My turn to enjoy the view."

"As you wish, my love."

They walked around the beach and Clint noting that once again, people were up early. The Haitian beach was quite crowded. There were many small cabanas, or "shells" set up for sunbathers to take a break from the sweltering heat. And it was definitely hot and humid. He'd been warned that the beaches here were rocky and shelly. He guessed the sand washed out with the tide and the heavier rocks and shells were all that remained. Still, it didn't stop people from flouncing around, although most wore some type of sandal or lightly padded shoes.

"They have ziplining, a tram tour, the beach, tropical drinks…" Clint felt Ransom's hand on his shoulder, the added warmth despite the heat.

"You're the expert. I trust you."

"Smart man."

Clint's thoughts now turned to what he would find out today

about Ransom. What were his secrets that he couldn't tell, but would be revealed here?

They walked for a while, leaving the beach and the crowd behind them, when Clint noticed some Haitians up ahead on the other side of a steel fence.

"Meesta, M'sieur, Pleeze, s'il vous plait! Fifteen or so pairs of hands reached out through the fence, the vocal begging continuous.

"What is that all about? Why are they there?" Clint asked.

"They are the locals, trying to coerce you into purchasing their wares."

"What is the fence for?"

"This Land is restricted and privately owned. It is for the strict use of the cruise ship company and their passengers."

"It seems kind of sad."

"The alternative would be constant harassment from the locals, and not only would cruise ships cease to visit here, but the Haitian economy would suffer greatly from the lack of tourist income. In addition, the Haitian government is paid a substantial income for the use of their land. Haiti is the poorest nation in the western hemisphere. The money that the tourists and the cruise ship companies bring in helps Haiti from becoming completely destitute."

"I had no idea. I live in L.A., and I think we have a homeless problem."

Ransom's face changed. "I know what you have been thinking all morning. It is time you learned it all. Follow me. It isn't much farther."

They walked off into a jungle-ish area and went along in silence for a few minutes. Clint's mind was inundated with dark thoughts and anxiety. *What is he going to tell me? Can I handle it? This must be bad. Why hasn't he told me? What's here in the middle of this jungle? Maybe he's going to leave me! No, stop it! You love him. Everything will be fine. Trust him!*

The trees opened up on an expanse. There were thatched huts similar to those on the beach area, and there were Haitians of all ages bustling around. It appeared to be a small village.

"This is a special village, with some special people. You are familiar with the voodoo religion?"

Clint was puzzled, but answered, "I know a little. I know it is a religion and not all about sticking pins into dolls and playing with venomous snakes."

"In this village voodoo is sacrosanct. You will find all of the beliefs and practices here. I visit here every voyage."

"And you... believe in it, practice it?"

"I do not practice. But over the many years I have definitely come to believe." He paused, deep in thought. "Believe, and perhaps... hope. Hope for redemption, forgiveness, mercy. Hope for... something else. A chance..."

Clint was now totally confused. *Redemption? For what? A chance?*

Ransom's mood and demeanor had completely changed. Clint saw regret and sadness on his handsome face. He wanted to hold him. He felt afraid for him.

A cloud passed overhead and darkened the area. Clint could feel the temperature drop. Strange.

"I have never brought anyone here. I need to share this with someone… you. So many years have passed… and here you are. Similar in certain ways… and then you brought the book. The memories—"

"I am so lost, Ransom." Clint had to stop him rambling. He needed answers. "I think you're the most amazing man. I am so in love with you. We had this crazy connection from the start—as "Hollywood" as that sounds. But redemption and mercy, and always talking about so many years… now voodoo! You've got to help me."

"I know. It's not right. I'm not being fair to you. Bringing you here is the only way I know to explain. You had to see for yourself… hear it. And even then you probably won't believe me."

"Ransom." Clint took his hand. "Coming from the land of lies and deception, I value the truth. For some insane reason, I've trusted you from the beginning. I've heard a lot of unbelievable stories before, I'm sure yours can't be that far-fetched." As he said it, he doubted his words. His instinct told him that he was about to hear something even Hollywood hadn't imagined.

He watched Ransom's eyes mist over as he said, "Thank you. I hope you mean that." He leaned in and kissed Clint so tenderly that he thought he felt the kiss in his soul.

Clint eased away, breaking the bond. "Tell me."

Ransom took his hand and led off a ways to a small, isolated hut, smaller than most of the others. Before he could knock on the door, an accented, angelic voice came from inside, "Enter Capitaine Ransom and friend."

They pushed the fragile door open. "Bonjour, Ransom." An exotic-looking and exotically clad woman with long, flowing dark hair sat on a thatched chair on the far side of the room—for it was no more than that: a room. A room surrounded with of candles of varying sizes. A small, round, wooden table was placed before her. On it were more candles and several vials of opaque liquids. An earthenware bowl sat in the middle.

"Bonjour, Anaisa," Ransom said, nodding his head, almost bowing. "This is Clinton Porter."

"Ah oui. Tres bien. Tres beau." She smiled slyly.

"Thank you... uh, merci." Clint thanked God for working six months in Provence on that Louis Malle film. He'd learned a few words and phrases, like: tres beau—very handsome

"Pleeze. Seet down." Her voice had an odd musical quality.

Clint looked at the woman and noticed two thatched stools on the opposite side of the table from her. Had they been there before? He looked around the hut again, noting a small sleeping area with a straw mat and some recessed areas with pots, bottles, more vials, and an assortment of containers. Great set decoration. There had to be thirty or more lit candles, and he wondered why it wasn't hotter than hell in here, or why she didn't fear burning the place down.

Ransom escorted him to the stools and sat.

Up close, Clint couldn't determine Anaisa's age. Her beauty, however, was indisputable: her skin flawless and richly tanned, or maybe it was natural. Her eyes were black and seductive. As he looked into her eyes, he felt himself grow warmer, and he knew it wasn't from the candles. Her sexuality was unnerving, hypnotic.

"Thees is the man, Ransom." Her voice had a finality to it. "After all these years… you have found him." Her smile became warm and she nodded. "So like heem… and yet not."

So like who? Clint became concerned, and not a little leery. What had he walked into? "Like who?" he said.

"You have not told heem?" She looked at Ransom, who shook his head.

"Heez lover, Mel."

A pained, wistful look came over Ransom's face. "He was my first mate."

"A sweet boy, young, nice looking." Anaisa's eyes locked on Clint's. "But you are much better looking."

Clint felt the heat from her sexuality again. "What happened to him?"

She glanced over at Ransom. "He passed from this world many, many years ago."

Clint felt his chest tighten. What is happening here? Why is Ransom so silent?

Ransom leaned into her. "Anaisa, have you found anything at all that might help me. Anything that will break the curse?"

"Yemoja is the most powerful god of all of us. She eez the mother to the all the seas and living creatures. I beseeched her. She has tried to find another… but there are no more. You destroyed the last of their kind. They are exteenct." She drew out the last word.

Clint would have collapsed if he hadn't been sitting. Now he had another hundred questions and no answers. He couldn't stand it. He blurted out, "What the hell is going on?"

Ransom's felt held a new despair. "Somehow I had hoped… It doesn't matter. I'm so sorry, Clint. So sorry…" Tears streamed down his cheeks as he stared deeply into the candle's flame. Lost.

"Anaisa, please tell me what is going on! I can't take him looking like this. You have to help him"

"Ah, mon cher, eef only I could. I see how much you love each other. Eet ees not fair, as you say. Life, eet can be so cruel."

Ransom stood suddenly, and left the hut.

"Ransom, wait!" Clint called after him.

Anaisa put a hand on his arm to stay him. "No, let heem be. Thees is for him to deal with. He neeeds to be alone."

"But I want to be with him… help him." Clint let out a sob and looked at her. "Am I going to lose him?" Another sob. "I love him so much."

"I cannot say. He has lived for so long… hoping… Now I fear the despair ees too great."

"Can you please explain to me what happened? I need to know. Please just tell me. I don't care what it is; I'll believe you… I promise." He swallowed, stifling another sob.

"Very well. I weel tell you the tragedy of your Capitaine."

The light from the candles grew dimmer in the room, not

guttering, merely less luminous. Yet Anaisa kept her own luminosity. She took both of Clint's hands in hers. Once again, he felt the heat. She squeezed tightly then released him and leaned back.

Her voice grew husky. "You have heard the story of the great white whale?"

"*Moby Dick*," he said, recalling immediately reading the last sentence mere hours ago.

"Oui, the fiction story."

Clint's mind whirled. "Are you saying it's true?"

Anaisa stared, her serious countenance giving him his answer.

"It can't be!" he yelled. "A giant white whale. There aren't any. How—" He froze, mouth agape. "You said, 'They're extinct. You've destroyed the last of their kind.'"

"Oui, cher, Capitaine Ransom St. James is the infamous Capitaine Ahab."

"But that was a hundred and fifty years ago!"

"Oui."

Clint tried to organize in his mind what he was hearing. "The curse... How? What..."

"I weel explain it to you."

Clint drew in a long breath, knowing what he was about to hear would be the most fantastical tale, the likes of which Hollywood could only dream up.

"Ransom was the best, and most arrogant Capitaine of the seas. He would often make hazardous and foolish voyages. Typhoons were nothing to heem. He thought he was invincible. There was no challenge he would not accept. He was a legend and held een awe by all. Women and men wanted heem, envied him, adored him. He was always proving heez prowess and masculinity. Then he heard the tale of the white whale. A legend eetself. A demon. A monster. The most magnificent creature on earth. And Ransom had to conquer eet.

"Yemoja, goddess of the seas went eento a rage. Thees was her domain and her beloved creature. She swore to curse heem forever if he harmed her child.

"Ransom scoffed at her and said that no one could tell heem what he could or could not do. He would keel the beast.

"And as you know from the story een the book… he did.

"Yemoja cursed Ransom and his crew. His men were all keeled and your Capitaine Ransom was cursed to sail the seas for all eternity."

Clint sat in silence and awe, taking it all in and trying to make logical sense of it. There was no logical sense. One could not accept only part of the story; one had to accept it all. He stared at Anaisa and found himself nodding, and accepting. But Ishmael, or whatever his name was, he lived, like in the book?"

"Ah, oui, Eeshamel, sweet Mel, the Capitaine's lover, I saved heem weeth a love spell. That was all I could do against such a terrible curse. Yemoja is most formidable. Mel leeved, but I had also angered her with my spell, and she saw to eet that they never saw each other again. The only memory ees that book… *Moby Dick*."

Clint's eyes grew wide in recognition. "Ishmael—Mael—Mel. Melville! Herman Melville! Ransom's lover was Herman Melville?" he shouted in disbelief.

"Cleent." Anaisa's voice was soothing. "There are many things in life that you would say are unbelievable. You love heem very much." It was a statement.

"So much…" He started to cry in earnest. Through his tears he said. "I do look like him—Mel—don't I?"

"As a told you, a leetle. But he was a boy. You are a man.

Clint had to know. "Did he, Ransom… love him?"

"Ah, mon petit, you must understand thees love. It was adventure and excitement, first love. Thees is not the love you and your Capitaine have. Thees is the true love, eternal love—the love everyone wants to find, but so few do. Eet is the love that geeves me my power and strength as a goddess."

Clint wiped at his eyes. "Then… then you can help us?"

"I want to, more than you know, mon cher. I weel talk to Bokor, the sorcerer, who handles both the dark and the light, and to some of the other gods. Perhaps, there is something… I do not know. I do not want you to hope too much. I can beseech Yemoja once more, yet she is most bitter and does not forgive easily."

"Thank you. Thank you, Anaisa. I know you'll try." He put his hands on hers for comfort. "I have one more question. How is it that Ransom can go on land at times? We were on Grand Cayman and Cozumel…"

"I do not know the particulars of thees curse. Yemoja is sly and secretive. Ransom cannot die, but I am sure if he tried to defy her, his punishment would make him wish he were dead. But he ees a good man weeth a loving heart, as you have seen. What he did those many years ago was an act of folly and youth. Tragic, surely, but not unredeemable. After these many years, the whale would surely be dead. Perhaps, Yemoja will finally understand that. Ransom is no longer that arrogant youth. He has matured and realized his mistakes, learned humility. You are not wrong to love heem, Clint."

Clint could see in her eyes that she too loved him—not the way he did—but in her own way.

"We can but try," she said.

Clint sensed the hopeless undertone. It had been one hundred and fifty years ago. Why would Yemoja suddenly change her mind? For him.

He wanted to die. He had found the one person he wanted to spend his life with. His reason to live… and here was this… this insanity. This crazy impossible situation. There had to be something someone could do! He voiced his thought to her, "There has to be something—" His voice broke.

"Ah, mon pauvre petit, I weel not stop trying. I can see the extraordinary love you have. Eet ees in the air around you. And he loves you as fiercely, of that I am sure."

"Thank you," Clint choked out. "Please, Anaisa, I'll do anything, ANYTHING to have him. I can't…" He was crying hard now. "Can't… lose him." He put his head in his hands, shoulders shaking violently in concert with his sobbing.

Anaisa placed a hand on his shoulder.

Clint knew in that moment, with that touch, that he was in

the presence of a goddess. He could feel her empathy as she shared his pain… and his love. He didn't want to move, or even raise his head. He wanted to bask in this empathic symbiosis. He could feel her absorbing his anguish while simultaneously giving him her own ethereal love and sympathy. He took in a huge gasp of air and felt the rush of Anaisa, the goddess of love, fill every cell in his body. His entire being became focused into one image: Ransom. It was an explosion of sensation that made him bolt upright and break his contact with the goddess.

Everything at once became clear to him. He was inspired. Driven. He would find a way to break this damn curse. He would find it… or die trying. Ransom was his future. His destiny. Anaisa had shown him that.

Or maybe he had known it all along. And it was the clarity of that realization that Anaisa had shown him.

Love was unexplainable—paranormal. Why shouldn't the achievement of it be as well?

These thoughts made him think of Melville. Is that why *Moby Dick* had always seemed like a supernatural horror story? The mythical white whale. The fanatical, obsessed Ahab. Did Melville know all this? Had he loved Ransom the way he did?

His thoughts were interrupted with, "Een my millennia of exeestance, I have never seen a love as powerful as the one you have for your Capitaine. He ees a lucky man, mon cher. Perhaps it weel be enough." She looked upward over Clint's head, as if something had caught her attention.

"I will do whatever I have to do, Anaisa. I'll pray to Yemoja every day." Clint noted Anaisa's still off-focused gaze.

"She is aware."

Clint turned his head around, trying to see what the goddess was looking at. There was nothing. "Yemoja, please, I beg of you," Clint called to the air where Anaisa's eyes were focused. "Please tell me what I can do. What kind of prayer or sacrifice…" He knew he was blathering. Sacrifice? What am I thinking? "Please, Yemoja, there must be something…" He was crying again, but he didn't care; he didn't care about anything except saving Ransom.

All of the candles in the room guttered and went out. The small hut was pitch dark.

Then, as if by magic, for Clint assumed that's what it was, the candles relit and the hut reappeared.

"Yemoja hears your plea," Anaisa said.

"Yes, but will she help?" Clint knew he'd never sounded more desperate.

"There ees no knowing with Yemoja. She has heard you and that is something. I weel do all I can do. But the final decision is hers."

"I know, I know, but what do I do now? Clint felt the tears burning the backs of his eyes. He had never felt so desolate, so helpless.

"You must go to heem. He needs you now. Be weeth him and enjoy the time you are given."

"That's it?" Clint started to panic.

"Yes, mon cher." Her tone was soothing.

"But I want more than that! I want forever!"

"Hush, mon petit. If it ees meant to be…" Her voice trailed away, Clint not hearing her final words, as she bowed her head. Then: "Go now. Find heem. For he aches as much as you do. Go… now."

Clint nodded to the bowed head, sniffed hard, rubbed his eyes, felt the burning irritation from his tears. He pulled his hands away.

She was gone.

"Anaisa?"

"Go to heem, mon cher," he heard in the air around him.

* * *

He found Ransom on the edge of the village, sitting on the ground, elbows on knees, staring at the harbor in the distance.

"Now you know everything," Ransom said, keeping his eyes on the distant ocean. "I will understand if you hate me. You should. I lied to you. I deserve your loathing. I never should have done this to you. You…" His voice choked off abruptly. He swallowed and continued, "You don't deserve this. What I have done is… is—"

"Stop! Stop it." Clint realized he was crying… again. What was up with him? L-O-V-E. He was in love. Only something so powerful and wonderful could make him feel so weak. He'd finally found it, and he'd be damned if he was going to lose it! If this was going to be the fight of his life, then he was ready to give it up for this incredible man. "I love you."

Ransom's head snapped around. Clint saw the anguished look. The tears. (He wasn't the only one.) The love. His eyes welled up and burned. He had to get control. The problem was: he was out of control in love with this man.

"Please…" Ransom's breathing was heavy. He gulped for air. A whisper escaped his throat. "Please… don't love me."

Clint's throat closed, but he managed to say, "Too late."

In a flurried rush, Ransom had his arms locked around Clint, holding him so hard Clint could barely breathe.

"Ransom…"

"Just let me hold you," Ransom said.

Clint hugged him back with all his heart.

They stayed that way for a while, until Ransom eased up on his crushing bear-hug, and pulled back to look at Clint, wet tears mingling with dried. "I do not deserve a man like you—as much as I want you. I do not deserve you." His voice was raspy. "Even though I have to let you go, I don't want to. Not ever."

Clint swallowed. "Anaisa is going to try to talk with the other gods again, and maybe this time they can convince Yemoja to remove the curse. I prayed to Yemoja, and she heard my plea. Anaisa told me she did."

"Yemoja heard you?" Clint caught the slight hope in his voice. "Maybe there is a chance. She has not paid me heed in all these many years."

"I believe it. I have to. There is no life for me without you,

Ransom. How can She not see what a fine man you are? That you've changed?"

"I do not know. But I do know you have changed me." He put his hands on either side of Clint's face. "And no matter what happens, knowing you, loving you, and being loved by you is the most wonderful thing that has ever happened to me. And if I am doomed to sail the seas for eternity, alone, I will always have this one week of perfect bliss to remember and hold in my heart." His tears of love flowed, and he leaned down and gave Clint a kiss so tender he thought his heart would break.

Pulling his lips from Clint's he whispered, "I love you."

Clint couldn't speak. He wanted time to freeze. He wanted this moment to be his last, for nothing could be better. He reached and grabbed one of Ransom's hands, which still held his face. He brought it to his lips and kissed it. "Thank you." He turned, still clutching Ransom's hand, and they walked back to the ship in silence, each, both looking forward to their last night together... and their possible future.

* * *

Two Months Later

Labadee, Haiti

6:00 P.M.

Ransom watched the last two passengers re-board the Windjammer. "You almost missed the boat, as they say. You gents get caught up in the island's pleasures?"

"You might say that," said a brawny, thirty-something blond man, and he slapped the ass of the, even blonder, early twenty-something at his side.

Ransom smiled, always a little wistfully now, whenever he observed affection between his guests. How he missed Clint.

Communication between them these past months had been sparse. And every time a phone communication was made, the call would drop, as if something or someone didn't want them to communicate. He assumed it was part of his curse. Clint was the first person he had ever tried to contact after a voyage. So, like his limited time on land, any outside contact also appeared to have its limits.

But he had his memories, and they were just as real and vivid as when they'd made them. He closed his eyes and imagined touching Clint's hard muscled chest, his smooth broad shoulders. He breathed in, and he could smell Clint's skin redolent with the salty air and sun-burnished sweat.

He felt himself stir. He opened his eyes. He needed to calm down. It wouldn't do for the captain to be walking around the ship's guests with a hard-on. Although, given the current slew of passengers, he'd fit right in. This group always seemed to be horny. He'd seen more open nudity on this trip than on any other, which didn't help him at all. He didn't desire any of the men, who had not been shy about wanting to have sex with him. It only increased his desire to be with the one he could never have again.

He realized, now, that he had lied when he'd told Clint that their one week together would last him, and that he would rather have had their one week than not to have known him.

Tennyson was a fool. Better to have loved and lost... What a load of crap. Lord Alfred should have known better. His In Memoriam to his friend Arthur Hallam could not have been more homoerotic.

Why was he thinking these odd thoughts?

Clint. That's why.

He missed him so much. If he couldn't have him, why couldn't he die? This was the cruelest punishment of all. How Yemoja must still despise him. He could almost hear her vengeful laughter. The ultimate torture: give a taste of what could have been.

His tears began. He cried so often now it was getting to be routine—at least once a day. He looked off into the beautiful azure Caribbean and let them flow, the soft balmy breeze drying them on his cheeks. This wasn't a curse: This was hell.

He walked along the corridor to his cabin, his tread slow and plodding. This was a bad day—one of his worst since Clint had left him. His mind stirred with thoughts of Clint, forgetting him and finding someone else. Someone else to share his bed—share his life. They would grow old together and die. "While I go on living forever!" he yelled aloud and pounded his fist into the hall's wood paneling. He stood, staring at the wall, enjoying his throbbing hand. The pain. He wanted to feel something—anything—besides this agonizing despair. He sank to his knee; his head followed to the floor.

A cabin door opened. A well-built, fortyish, nearly naked man stepped out. "Anything wrong," the man said. "I heard a crash or something." He took a couple of steps. "Captain? Are you all right?" He reached out a hand.

Ransom raised his head. "I'm fine. I tripped. Embarrassing, actually, being the captain. Thank you." He took the man's hand and rose to his feet.

"If you'd like to come into my cabin. I could give you a massage to make you feel better, relieve the aches, make sure you didn't hurt anything. I'm a professional masseuse."

Ransom looked at the man: the strong, heavily muscled body; the lustful look in his eyes; the growing interest in his barely there briefs. "Perhaps later. I need to dress for dinner. It's optional formalwear tonight. But as the captain, I always opt for formal. And I need to make sure I'm there to greet you all for cocktails in a few minutes. Formal or casual for you?"

The man was nonplussed. Ransom guessed he wasn't used to being rejected. Well, he was good-looking.

"What would you like me to wear, Captain? I have both." The man's ego had obviously not been bruised too much, and he flexed his pectorals to prove it.

"Formal, I think. Nothing sexier than a man in a tuxedo." He hoped that would assuage the man's ego. He didn't want to be rude.

"And it's so much fun to take it off the other guy later on."

"Touché. See you for cocktail hour then."

"You know it, Cap." The man clamped a hand on Ransom's

ass and squeezed hard. "Nice glutes, Cap. See you soon. The name's Max, by the way."

Ransom flinched slightly as Max released his death-grip on his left cheek. "Max." He nodded and walked by the man to his cabin.

"Sweet ass," trilled Max, right before Ransom reached his cabin.

He opened the door.

"About time."

Ransom blinked twice, then a third time.

Clint.

It couldn't be. "Clint? How?"

"Yes, Ransom."

Clint lay on Ransom's bed, fully clothed. But he couldn't have been more desirable if he'd been stark naked. He felt himself grow warm with desire and... love. Dear Lord, how he loved this man. It was an exquisite torture seeing him: the man who had haunted his thoughts and dreams every minute for these past two excruciating months. He'd resigned himself to never seeing him again. Yet, here he was. He blinked hard a final time.

"Yes, I'm really here, Ransom, and if you don't get over here and kiss me right now, I'm going—"

But he didn't have time to finish before Ransom covered his mouth with his own hungry lips.

Ransom couldn't stop himself. He mauled and ravished Clint. He was a starving lion or shark with the fever of bloodlust. His saving grace was that Clint seemed to be as bloodlust hungry as he was.

They ripped at each other's clothing, buttons flew, cloth tore. At last, when the last vestige of clothing was gone, their scalding bodies melded. Hands and mouths were everywhere.

It was savage.

It was wonderful.

Maybe the gods didn't hate him so terribly after all. This reprieve of bliss was more than he could have hoped for. Maybe, hopefully, (he silently prayed), Clint would stay for a few days with him. A few days, that was all he would dare ask.

Clint.

His Clint.

He thought he would burst with the love inside him.

"Are you all right?" Clint broke his reverie.

"All right, can't begin to describe what I'm feeling. Why?"

"You're... crying."

Ransom hadn't even been aware of it. He wiped his cheek. "So I am." He wiped his other cheek. "I know this isn't fair of me to say, but it's you. You, Clint. My Love. You make me cry. You bring out a depth of feeling in me that I didn't think was possible. These are tears of blissful joy and happiness." He brought Clint in for a long, hard kiss. They broke apart and he continued, a touch of melancholy colored his voice, "Fate is cruel, my love. It gives a taste of what could be then snatches it away."

He stared deeply into Clint's eyes, their naked, sweating

bodies pressed close. "I will never love another as I do you." He felt the tear run down his cheek this time. "I only wish—" his throat closed off and he couldn't finish.

"Wish what, Ransom? Wish what? Clint brushed the errant tear from the handsome face and brought it to his lips.

Ransom burst out, "Wish that you could stay with me forever!" He gave a small sob. "I'm sorry, I shouldn't have said it, but it's how I feel."

Quietly, Clint said, "Is it, Ransom? Is it truly what you want?"

"More than anything in my very long life." He put his head on Clint's shoulder and let his tears flow, not caring, just enjoying the feel of his soulmate's warmth.

"I have to tell you something, then." Ransom started to raise his head. "No, just listen." He pushed Ransom's head back down.

"When I left you two months ago, I couldn't eat, sleep, think. You were all that consumed me. I had to find a way back to you, to be with you, to break the damn curse. I went to New Orleans and spoke with some Voodoo practitioners there. I told them everything. They, an old man and woman—he was a priest; she was some kind of priestess—were so understanding and sympathetic. They contacted Bokor, the Voodoo god—very powerful. He can make zombies and does things with the dead. But even he couldn't help. They gave me a suggestion, something I might try. I had to be very certain, though, and there was no guarantee, She, Yemoja, would go for it.

"They sent me back here to Haiti to see Anaisa. That's why

I'm here. I told Anaisa what Bastian and Bastienne—those were the old couple's names—suggested I do. They told me that if Yemoja's curse on you could not be broken, then maybe she could…" He swallowed. "…curse me too, so that I could be like you. Forced to sail… forever."

Ransom squeezed Clint so hard he made him grunt. He leaned his head back and looked up. He saw fear in Clint's eyes, but underneath that, he also saw love. "Would you?" he whispered.

Clint returned the whisper. "Would you want me to?"

Ransom wanted that more than anything, but instead of saying so, he said, "I could never ask that."

Clint's voice rose. "It's not your decision. I need to know if that's what you want."

He couldn't lie. His future might rest on his next words. "I've prayed to God—all the gods—every day, to be with you forever."

Clint's eyes changed. All the fear and anxiety was gone.

All that was left was unadulterated love.

Ransom watched the blue eyes fill. Clint said, "I have prayed for the same."

"You would do this for me?"

"For us," Clint said, bringing a hand up to brush Ransom's jaw.

"Yemoja will agree? She will do this?"

"She already has." Clint held his breath.

Ransom could no longer maintain his emotions, not that he was doing a very good job of it as it was. He pulled Clint into him and hugged him fiercely. And hugged. And… cried. His entire body shook as the tears streamed and his pent-up feelings released. Decades of anguish poured out of him, and Clint held him tight.

Ransom didn't know how long he cried and he didn't care.

When he was finally finished, he wiped his tears from Clint's soaked shoulder and chest, relishing the feel of the smooth muscles.

His.

Forever.

"Forever," he said aloud.

Clint had remained silent the entire time he'd cried. Now Ransom ventured a look at him. He noticed Clint's own tear-stained cheeks. One last question: "Do you have any regrets?"

"If I ever did, which I didn't, this last hour removed any of them." He smiled softly.

"I cried for an hour?"

"Or so… but you needed to. And what is an hour, my incredible Captain, when we have eternity?"

Ransom answered the loving smile with one of his own. "Indeed, my love, eternity."

OPHIUCHUS

Ophiuchus-The Serpent Bearer

Traits: Seeker of knowledge and wisdom, dreams and premonitions, flashy dresser, jealous, wanderer, curious, passionate, charismatic, attracts good luck, driven, critical, secretive, eccentric, honest.

I am so glad that's over. "God, what a prick!" Riley Miller
realized he'd just said this aloud. He looked around the crowded
terminal at the other passengers who were waiting patiently for the
plane to arrive and take them away from the "Big Apple."

Riley had never liked New York City, and was only here now
because he'd come to break it off with Chad, who, come to find out,
was already living with someone else! I should've made him pay for
my plane ticket. Why couldn't he have told me a long time ago?
He'd been seeing this guy for months—and me too, at the same time!
I hope the other guy gets a clue and leaves him. He wasn't that good
in bed anyway. Too selfish. I don't know why I bothered. I'm not
desperate. I'm only thirty-six, decent-looking. I hit the gym four or
five times a—

"Excuse me." Riley's self-analyzing was interrupted by a
pleasant male voice. "Do you mind if I sit here? There doesn't appear
to be much available seating."

"Sure. No problem. I shouldn't have had my bag here
anyway." Riley grabbed his carry-on from the seat next to him and
shoved it between his legs on the floor, then looked up into the most
stunning pair of emerald-green eyes he'd ever seen. "Wow! Great
eyes."

The man smiled broadly.

"Shit. That was rude. I'm really sorry." Riley tried to backpedal. "I don't usually blurt out—"

"It's quite all right. And thank you. Your eyes as well, are also a rather intriguing silver-blue, and with your dark hair you are Black-Irish, I presume?"

Riley was nonplussed. This hot guy is gay? Must be. He complimented my eyes. "Uh, yeah. I'm Riley Miller." He proffered his hand.

"Roark Lennox."

The man's grip was firm, and when their hands met, Riley got a sense of deja vu, a feeling of having met this man before... but knowing he hadn't. He definitely would have remembered this intensely, sexually attractive man. Still... Riley felt the man's hand getting warmer. It made Riley warmer as well. "Going to Vegas, I take it?" He needed to know more about Roark. Other than his good looks, the perfectly cut, short-cropped, dirty-blond hair and startling eyes, there was something intriguing on a deeper level. It was only a first impression, but Riley always trusted his gut—sometimes it even paid off: like taking the baseball scholarship to a smaller school had still gotten him noticed by the majors and he made it into the big leagues—in a big way. Two world series championships. A great life. A dream life. So far.

He didn't know what was next, but his gut told him it would be something extraordinary. That's why he'd retired from the game. It was time. He needed to be ready for the next chapter in his life. Maybe this guy, Roark, was it? All his senses were on alert.

"Yes, I live there. Well, at least I have a house there. I travel so frequently, I'm not sure where home is."

His emphasis on "home," made Riley think that he was also searching for something. "You travel?" he asked Roark.

"Yes. Too much, I fear. I have what you would call wanderlust. I am returning now from a month in Nepal."

"Nepal? Whoa. How was that? What were you there for? A whole month? What did you do? Was it cold? Did you climb Mount Everest? You look fit enough to."

Roark was laughing hard. "I infer you are the inquisitive type. Let me see... Yes, Nepal. Quite fascinating. Possible enlightenment and understanding. A whole month, though I, perhaps, should have stayed longer. I also explored the area. Rested. And asked many questions. And... yes, even in summer, it was rather chilly. And no, I did not climb Mount Everest." He thought for a moment. "I believe I answered all of your questions."

"Not hardly. And I'm sorry I threw all that at you. I never knew anyone who went to Nepal. I think I'd like to see it. It's always seemed like one of those mysterious, forbidden places, like Borneo or Bhutan. Thanks for indulging me."

"Not at all. It's refreshing to meet someone so curious and excited. Your elan is infectious. I like you, Riley Miller. I would like to get to know you better, I think."

"I would like to get to know you too, Roark Lennox."

"It is almost six," Roark said, glancing at his watch. "Shall we get a drink? I see the bar isn't too crowded yet, and it's right here."

"Uh, Roark? We have a plane to catch."

"It's delayed," Roark said without hesitation.

"No, it's not. The board said it was on time. They would have announced it."

"Attention all passengers on Flight 701 to Las Vegas. There has been a delay. We will notify you when the craft is ready to board. Thank you for your patience."

Riley listened to the announcement, while staring at Roark. He continued to stare as the announcement was repeated in Spanish. "How did you know?"

"I get these feelings, a sixth sense, if you will. Does that bother you?"

"Hell, no! I think it's cool." They entered the bar and sat on stools at the end. The bartender met them there and they ordered. "Did you develop that in Nepal? Or have you always been psychic?"

"You amaze me, Riley," Roark said, shaking head. "Have you always been so trusting?"

Their drinks were set before them.

"That was fast. So, by trusting, you mean gullible? I like to think I'm not, but when I meet someone I'm attracted to, I want to believe them." Sipping his Jameson's, he continued, "It's a good thing you knew we'd be delayed. This place is already starting to get packed now." He surveilled the bar, observing the rapidly growing line of customers jockeying for a position at the bar to order drinks. They'd chosen stools at the far end, away from the center of the mob.

He sipped again. "I wonder how long the delay is? Or maybe

you already know?' He clinked his glass to Roark's and winked.

"Funny you should mention that." Roark's voice lowered. "Actually, there's nothing humorous in what I'm about to tell you."

"You got serious real fast. Is this bad?"

"Extremely. And I hope you meant what you said about trusting me."

"All right. Lay it on me."

Roark took a healthy sip of his cocktail. "I have dreams—prescient dreams. They are vivid and ofttimes unnerving. Last night was the most unnerving one yet."

Riley quietly sipped his whiskey and waited, a little unnerved himself. His attention completely focused on Roark, all other distractions obliterated.

"I dreamed I would meet you here. That our plane would be delayed. That we would drink together at this bar, on these very stools." He took a large gulp, finishing his drink. He looked around, then leaned in close to Riley. "I saw our plane crash near the Grand Canyon."

Riley blinked once. His thoughts roiled. His stomach clenched. He tossed back the rest of his drink. "What can we do?"

"About the plane? Nothing. It is fate. There is nothing to say to convince the airline not to proceed with the flight. In this day and age, I would be arrested and questioned, and definitely put on the 'No Fly' list. At the very least."

Riley contemplated it all. He knew Roark was right. They were helpless. They couldn't even tell the other passengers without causing some type of panic, which would result in the same consequences. Then he said, "Can we change our flight?"

"Yes."

"All these other people..."

"We can only choose our own destinies. Their kismet is theirs. Someone will be on that flight."

"So, your dreams only tell of possible futures. They're not the absolute future." Riley realized it was a statement/question.

Roark rescued him. "Dreams are meant to be interpreted; they aren't predictions, as such."

"Right, not your first time at the rodeo."

"Hardly. Mind you, this isn't a nightly occurrence. The dreams are sporadic. I can go months without any significant dreaming."

"So, you can't influence them?"

"No. And some of them are positive."

"You don't just dream of death and disaster. That's good to know."

Roark gave him a wry look. "Still want to know me better?"

"More than ever," Riley said, and signaled the bartender for another round. "It's really, I don't know, frustrating, emasculating to know there's nothing we can do. Depressing."

"It does help me to realize that catastrophes such as these can have a positive effect."

"I don't see it."

"The people involved, friends, family, co-workers, will all be affected. For most, it will open their eyes to the fragility of life, and what a true blessing and treasure it is. These events change people; and most times for the better. They will appreciate their lives more and those they love. Often the most disagreeable and seemingly uncaring people do a reversal of personality. I'm not a polemicist; this has been my observation over the years."

"I get it. When I think about what you're saying and apply it to my own life, losing my parents, etc, and how other people I've known have been affected by death it makes sense. Like those platitudes: 'What doesn't kill you makes you stronger,' 'Every cloud has a silver lining—'

"Exactly." Roark nodded fervently. "Once I came to terms with my 'gift,' I began to realize its significance and potential. Don't get me wrong, the severity of this particular tragedy is more than daunting, but I have to maintain my perspective, and I have to remember that I am not a god who can make decisions for others."

Riley gave a quizzical look. "Is there a chance that by us changing our flight we could be altering some outcome?"

"It already has, Riley. We will not be a part of the death toll."

"Right." He slammed back the rest of his fresh drink and said, "Shots. We need shots. I need to not think about this whole plane-crash, destiny thing. I'm going to try and forget I know about it, and pray you're wrong." He shook his head. "God, I hope you're wrong. Then, I guess, we'll see what other flights there are to Vegas."

"You're still going?" Roark raised an eyebrow.

"If you are? I'm hook, line and sinkered. I knew the next

chapter in my life was going to be something extraordinary; I just didn't realize how extraordinary. To you: O great seer." He handed Roark the magically delivered shot and raised his own glass in toast.

They downed the shots and were instantly refilled.

"I would marry our bartender, if she was he," Riley said, and put his hand on Roark's knee, then leaned into him.

Roark responded, "I wouldn't tell her that, if you want to keep her 'amazing service.' I believe she has designs on you."

"Good point. I probably shouldn't squeeze your knee or kiss you either. Whoops! And I probably shouldn't have said I want to kiss you either... I think I need the men's room." He got up a trifle unsteadily and wandered off.

When he returned, there were fresh drinks and shots on the bar.

"Kelsey's treat," Roark said before Riley could ask. "She's from Newport, Rhode Island, just graduated Columbia, for acting. Single, also a Leo."

"Does she like moonlight walks on the beach and old movies?" Riley quirked a corner of his mouth.

"Didn't get that far. She had other customers. But you may ask her when she returns, if you'd like."

"Maybe later. I'd rather know what you like."

"Truly?"

"Truly." Riley picked up Roark's drink and handed it to him. "Since we haven't re-booked our flights yet."

"All done. While you were exploring the pulchritudinous

wonders of the John Fitzgerald Kennedy Airport, I took the liberty of doing that. I hope you don't mind; and there were still two seats in First Class."

"I don't mind. I was gone that long? And how did—"

"Your ticket was in the outer flap of your bag. Yes, you were gone a while. The ticket is my treat. It's the least I can do for, as they say, 'rocking your world.'"

"That's too generous. And you probably saved my life!" He looked around quickly making sure no one had heard his outburst. He lowered his voice. "I don't know if I can ever repay that."

The air became heated as their eyes met. Both of them knowing what kind of "repayment" there could be.

"You're welcome." Roark broke the moment. Raising a glass, he said, "My turn. To you, Riley Miller. I feel my own world 'rocking' by the minute. I am at the precipice, waiting... waiting for... you?"

"I have to do this." Riley leaned in and pressed his mouth to Roark's.

Roark opened his mouth to Riley.

"Oh shit."

The men parted lips and looked in the direction of the voice.

Behind the bar, hands on hips, lips in a frustrated moue, was Kelsey, their bartender. "And just when I figured out who you were. All the good ones are gay!" She stalked away to the other side of the bar.

"I guess no more free drinks," Riley quirked a grin.

"Excellent conjecture," Roark quirked a similar smile. "And

precisely, who are you?"

"Oh, well, I played baseball."

"I surmise, professionally?"

"Yeah, a few years, mostly with the Cards—Cardinals. I'm retired. Riley picked up their shots and thrust one at Roark. "Down the hatch, Roark. We'll be paying for the rest... unless there's a shift change and we get somebody from our team." He tapped Roark's glass. "To the shortest, hottest kiss I've had in a long time." He brought the glass to his lips, then stopped. "There's lots more where that one came from." He winked and downed the shot.

A couple of hours later, they were seated on the plane, champagne in hands, more than a little bleary-eyed, but relaxed.

Riley was glad for the alcohol numbing his brain from the thoughts of the imminent crash of their other flight. He rationalized the inevitable, and tried to focus on the positive side of his meeting Roark. "I don't do First Class often," he said. "It seems like a waste of money... but right now it seems like the best investment ever— even if it is your money." He sipped the champagne. "Thank you, Roark."

He leaned into the handsome man on his right. He'd lost count of the number of times he'd given these small kisses to Roark over the past few hours. He hadn't cared who seen them in the bar— of course, the alcohol had helped that. He only knew he wanted a lot more of them, and ones that lasted alot longer. He was glad the lights in the cabin were dim. Now he slid his tongue into Roark's mouth and explored, giving the man the kind of kiss he'd wanted to all night.

Roark responded hungrily, seemingly just as pent up as Riley. They kissed until—

"Ahem," came from the male flight attendant—who was obviously on their team, and had been more than attentive from the moment they'd boarded—as he fanned himself. "You boys need to buckle up for takeoff." He pointed to their laps. "Don't hurt anything with the buckles." He smirked. "If you'd like I can help make sure they're secured."

"Would you?" Riley said, moving his arms wide.

"My pleasure." The attendant, whose name tag said Philip, leaned over and clipped the seatbelt over Riley's hips and obvious erection. Philip looked upward and uttered. "There is a God." his eyes met Riley's. "Thank you Mr. Miller. You were always my favorite baseball player. No one wore the uniform better."

"Thank you, Philip. And it's Riley. And if you would just top off our glasses for us that would be great."

"Right away, Mr…. Riley." Philip smiled demurely, gave a little bow, and scurried off.

Before Roark could speak, Riley said, "that was too much, wasn't it? Couldn't be the alcohol talking, could it? I'm really sorry. I'm not usually so crude. You—"

"Stop. You needn't apologize. I'm sure you made his flight memorable and have given something to brag about for years. How many men can say, 'I touched the great Riley Miller's penis?' I'm sure the story will be embellished, and a year from now it will include you being naked, fellatio, and the 'Mile high Club.'"

Riley laughed. "Wow, you're really something, Roark. You talk like an English professor; you drink like a sailor; you're in great shape, hotter than fu—shit. I mean, you're hot. An incredible kisser—"

"I think that's quite enough. And I am glad the lights are dim, as I'm blushing more than I can ever recall."

"Which is also hot." Riley leaned over again and planted another kiss.

"More champagne?" Philip.

The men's lips parted.

"I didn't mean to interrupt, but we're about to take off. Otherwise, I could have watched you all night." Philip immediately realized his gaffe, and tried to recover. "I mean... I... didn't want to disturb you."

"It's all right, Philip," Roark said, setting his glass on his right thigh. "You may top us off."

Riley noted the intentional setting of Roark's glass on the thigh farthest away from Philip, and noticed Philip trying to steady his hand as he poured, being careful to keep his eyes on the glass and not Roark's very full crotch. He wasn't successful, but he didn't spill either.

"Thank you, Philip. That's enough. I don't believe there's any more room in the glass."

"Right. You're welcome. Riley?"

"It's full. But later. Thank you," Riley said.

"Safe take off, gentlemen." And off he went.

Riley nodded his head. "Nice, Roark. You're full of surprises."

"Predictability is enervating." Roark maneuvered his lips to the over-filled flute and sipped it down to a safe-for-take-off level.

"I think you're the least enervating person I've ever met. If you were a pitcher, I'd say it was your change-up and not your fastball that I had to worry about."

"An apt analogy."

They chatted for a while after they took off, until Riley found himself nodding from the day, the stress, and the drink. He laid his head on Roark's shoulder, saying, "Just a few quick winks..."

"Ahem. Gentlemen, we're preparing to land. I have to take your glasses now and return the trays inside the seat arms." Philip leaned in, and with a conspiratorial whisper said, "You can leave your seats reclined if you'd like."

Two very groggy voices said, "Thank you."

The men's heads rose from each other's shoulders.

"Good morning," Roark said.

"If you say so," Riley managed. "Although, I liked sleeping on you, I could have done without the waking up part. I feel like shit."

Two hands were thrust under their noses. The hands held two glasses with very red liquid in them. "Bloody Marys, with my special non-hangover ingredient." Fill 'em up Philip.

"Thank you, Philip." Roark sniffed the glass.

"Drink them quickly. I'm supposed to be seated already."

The two men looked at each other, gave a "what the hell look," and drained their glasses.

"Wow, that was delicious," Riley said. "What's the special ingredient?"

"Pickle juice and crushed aspirin. We're not supposed to administer drugs to passengers. This way I didn't technically give the pills to you."

"You're a lifesaver. Thanks, Philip." Riley handed over his glass. "Hey, give me your address and I'll send you an autographed baseball."

"Oh-my-God! Really? That would be fabulous! I don't suppose you have a picture too I could display with it?"

"Sure, no problem. In my uniform? Or I might have one from that underwear campaign I did..."

"Yes! Yes! Both! If I could... I mean... That photo of you in your und—"

"Flight crew please prepare for landing in beautiful 'Lost Wages.'" The announcement cut off Philip's effusion.

"Sorry, sorry, but thank you, Riley. Thank you!" Philip squeezed Riley's biceps and scurried to his jumpseat, quickly strapping in.

"If that boy were older, I would have feared his having a heart attack," Roark muttered to Riley. "I'm beginning to think this furor you cause in people is the norm for you."

Riley felt himself redden. "Sometimes."

"Well, you are quite handsome, my athletic friend. Add to

that your celebrity, a revealing underwear ad, and you have a recipe for adoration."

Riley was hot now. "Can we talk about something else?"

"Your humility is quite charming as well. Now, before we begin our Las Vegas adventure, may I assume you are, hopefully, single?"

"I am. Officially, yesterday. Unofficially, it's been months. He found someone else but neglected to tell me. He was an asshole anyway. Selfish, egotistical. I mean, he was good-looking, but after you got to know him, his looks tarnished. And the long-distance thing wasn't working. He would never leave New York. And I hated it. So, it was going nowhere. The more I think about it, I don't know how I ever became involved with him. Crazy, huh?"

Roark looked slyly at him. "Maybe you were meant to break up at this time for a specific reason?"

Riley caught the innuendo. "Maybe. We'll see."

They walked into the terminal. There was a definite change in atmosphere. Everyone was talking. Riley noticed several faces filled with panic. He caught snippets of conversation and heard the words: "crashed," "died," "how many?"

"Roark." Riley gripped his arm hard and forced him to stop walking. "Roark, it happened. Like you said. All those people... It happened..."

"Yes, Riley, a terrible tragedy."

Riley felt himself getting dizzy. He released his death-grip on Roark's arm. His knees buckled and he fell to the ground.

"Riley!"

"Riley? Riley?" His eyes opened to the sound of Roark's concerned voice. "Riley, I'm here. You're all right. You passed out. It was only a few moments. Perhaps too much champagne, with the altitude..."

"Roark, no, I... It was the dream. Help me up."

Roark helped get Riley up and into a nearby chair. "What do you mean 'the dream?'"

Riley took a long deep breath. "It wasn' the booze. I suddenly remembered... I had a dream on the plane. It was the crash. I could see the pilot. He grabbed his head. Then... he slumped forward on the control panel. The co-pilot got up... helping... falling... hitting his head... Screaming. People flying through the aisles..."He put his hands over his face. "It was terrible—awful..."

Riley looked up at Roark and saw shock and... fear on his face. "What is it? Roark? What is it?"

Roark snapped out of his stupor. "It's nothing." He looked at Riley, and put his arm over his shoulder. "How horrible for you. To see that."

"But why did I see it?" His voice had an edge of panic to it. "I thought you were the one with the visions?"

Roark glanced around at the bustling terminal; everyone too pre-occupied to notice the two men. The sounds of slot machines and general white noise muffled their conversation. "I'm not certain. My guess is your subconscious took over after I told you my own premonition."

"Yeah, maybe. But it was so real. Like I was there watching it happen. It wasn't like any dream I've ever had before. I mean, I've had nightmares, but this was different. And the weirdest part is I didn't even remember it till you said something and the people around us started talking about it. Like a trigger or something. A switch. It's crazy, isn't it?" He looked at Roark, whose eyes seemed to be glazed over, unfocused. His body stiff. "Roark?"

"What you just said, a switch," Roark said, his gaze still fixed forward. "I had the same vision." He blinked, then turned to Riley and gave a small half-laugh. "My 'trigger' appears to have been delayed. I only remembered having the same dream after you started speaking of it. Riley Miller, kismet is an unfathomable concept." He moved his hand to Riley's knee, giving it a light squeeze. "Do you feel well enough to continue? It is a bit of a walk through the terminal. I could call for a wheelchair."

"No. I'm good. It was just such a shock. Like a blow to my brain." He put his hand over Roark's. "Uh, where are we going? Did we make a plan? Some of the conversation is fuzzy. But I do remember everything about the making-out part." He smiled and raised an eyebrow.

Roark laughed. "I guess you are feeling better. And my plan was to take you out to my house in Red Rock, if that is satisfactory. I have several bedrooms if you—"

"Great," Riley said, cutting off Roark as he stood. He pulled Roark up to him and whispered, "We'll have to try all of them out." He watched Roark's eyes become a deep emerald. "I see that meets with your approval."

"Most definitely."

* * *

"Wow, great place," Riley said, walking through the foyer into the great room. The sun shone in brilliantly through the wall of glass on the far side of the room. "The light is great. I love the arch over the window. Awesome couches." He caressed a cushion. "It's like buttery leather." He plopped down on the nearest one. "Whoa, they're even softer than they look. Come join me."

Roark moved to him and sat in the inviting arm Riley had opened for him. As he sat, Riley's arm came around his shoulders.

"You have great shoulders, hard, broad..." Riley squeezed hard. "Strong."

"Thank you. An excess of climbing, I fear, mountains, caverns..."

"You're some adventurer. Like a really hot Indiana Jones."

Roark was silent.

"Before you show me around the rest of this great place, can I ask you something personal?"

"Of course."

"I don't know how to ask without sounding stupid, so here goes. How come you're single? You are, right?" He didn't allow Roark to answer. "You're super smart, great body, great looking... Is it all the traveling?" He paused. "The visions?" He paused again.

"You know what, forget I asked. I do sound stupid. I'm rude. The only question you have to answer is the single part. I don't want to be a home-wrecker or get involved in some weird triangle; although maybe I should have asked this 3000 miles ago before we kissed and I latched onto you."

Roark leaned up and looked at Riley, his mouth quirking. "Yes, I am single."

"Thank God! That saved a lot of awkwardness."

Roark grinned wide. "As cliche as it sounds, I've never met anyone I wanted to be with forever. And I know that is what I'm looking for. I've never even lived with anyone. Of course the traveling hasn't made relationships conducive for anything long term. But it's more than that. I'm not certain I believe in destiny, but I do have this strong feeling, an intuition, if you will, that I am waiting for just one person. My soulmate. And that I will know when I find him."

"Have you had visions—premonitions about this?"

"If only..."

"Soooo... why me? Not that I don't want to be here, because I do. Very much. Do you think... ? Never mind. I'm doing it again. Show me the rest of your mansion." He stood and held out his hand to Roark.

"Thank you."

As they strolled, Riley gave his comments and opinions. "You designed all this? It's fantastic. It's so different but has a cohesive feel to it."

"Glad you like it."

"You're a man of many talents. A renaissance man. I can't wait to see your other talents." Riley let the innuendo linger in the air as he brushed his hand over a mosaic table top in the hallway before entering the kitchen. "Hey, do you have any food in this place. Or do you consider wine a food group?" He indicated the two large side-by-side wine refrigerators on the opposite side of the kitchen. "Not that that's a bad thing." He opened a refrigerator door and pulled out a bottle and examined a label. "Some of these wines look great."

"A very nice zinfandel. Yes, I also have food. I believe there are some steaks in the freezer and—"

Riley barreled over Roark's last words, Pleeease tell me you have a grill. Of course you must. You have everything. Good. Show me where it is. I'll do the steaks."

"Splendid. I will go to the store and get—"

Riley jumped in again, "Baked potatoes... asparagus! Grilled asparagus is my all-time favorite. I do a killer job of it."

Roark laughed. "I'm sure you do. I'll show you the grill. The steaks are in there on the left." He pointed to yet another refrigerator in the massive kitchen—a sub-zero this time. "I'll be back shortly. We can decant that wine." He pointed to the bottle Riley was still holding. "And it should be perfect with the steaks."

"Two would be more perfect." Riley said, and returned to the refrigerator to seek another bottle.

"Yes, you're right."

Riley pulled out another bottle and Roark proceeded to show

him around the kitchen: the various drawers and cupboards. Roark decanted the wine and poured them each a glass while he instructed Riley on the use of the grill.

"Great grill, and this zinfandel is fantastic," Riley said, finishing the glass.

"As it breathes more, the smoother it will become. Your next glass will taste even better."

"Fill 'er up." Riley handed his glass to Roark. "I love this patio too. Nice couches, a swing, and a fire pit! Perfect."

Roark handed the refilled glass to Riley. "I'll decant the other bottle before I run to the store for the vegetables and potatoes. Do you want anything else?"

"Dessert. Something chocolatey and gooey." He took a sip of the new glass of wine. "This is better. Wow. Or maybe something coconutty... Oh, I know: pineapple upside-down cake. If not, Boston cream pie."

Roark chuckled. "At least you've given me options."

"I like everything. Everything." He took another sip, looking over the lip at Roark to make sure he got the implication.

"Duly noted." Roark said. "I'll try to hurry before you've finished all the wine."

"Don't worry. If I run out, I know where to get more. I think you've got enough to tide me over." He took a large gulp, then smiled. "There is more of this, right?"

"There should be a least a case. I usually by it that way when I find a bottle I like."

"That's all?"

Roark chuckled again. "I'll hurry."

Riley lit the grill, and with wine in hand, decided to explore the house more intimately. He noted the lack of any personal photos. He stared out the floor-to-ceiling windows of the master bedroom. There was an incredible view of the Red Rock valley. The setting sun burnished the rocks and the shadows made the vista seem even more vast and spectacular. "Beautiful place, but where is the man?"

"Right here."

Riley turned abruptly and some of the red liquid sloshed onto his hand. "Shit! I didn't hear you. I don't think I spilled any on the floor, just my hand." He put his hand to his mouth and licked it off.

Roark moved to him. "Allow me." He pulled Riley's hand to his mouth and slowly licked his fingers, taking each one into his mouth and sucking on the digits, teasing them with his tongue.

Riley held his breath while he enjoyed the most erotic sensations on his fingers he'd ever had. He felt his below-the-belt digit growing hard.

Roark licked his palm.

"Aah!" Riley felt as if he'd been burned.

"I think I got it all," Roark said kissing his palm. "A mildly salty tang added to the vintage."

"Where did you learn to do that?"

"Just now. The opportunity presented itself and I took advantage. I hoped you wouldn't mind."

"Mind? You just blew my mind. That was amazing, and so

hot. What do you do for an encore?"

"I have some ideas, and a thirty-year-old Port which I think you will enjoy a swell."

"Do we have to wait?"

"Patience, my baseball-playing friend. A wonderful meal, some more of this fine wine—which has now become my favorite— a little dessert..."

"I get the picture. You're trying to seduce me. Well, consider me seduced, Professor. Hey, are you a professor?"

"I have studied: archaeology, ancient history, anthropology. I have a degree in all of them, but academia has never interested me. I have always been a doer. A seeker of the truth, the unknown and arcane."

"So professor isn't too far off the mark. You just don't teach. You're even more than Indiana Jones. They should make a movie series about you. You even look like a rugged movie star." He leaned in and kissed Roark.

Roark opened his mouth and passionately returned the kiss.

"And you kiss like a porn star." Riley wiped his mouth. "Let's eat."

They sat in the small formal dining room. The steaks finished. The wine finished. Port freshly poured.

Riley took a sip of the deep ruby liquid. "Amazing. As was the food and conversation." He raised the small Port glass to Roark. "But mostly the conversationalist."

Roark toasted in return. "It takes two."

They sipped.

"Would you like to watch the sunset with me? Tonight is the summer equinox, and as it is the longest daylight of the year, it should be setting shortly."

"Love to. Can we bring the Port? We might need another bottle too. This one's kinda small."

They got up from the table and made their way to the back patio. Riley interjected, "You still need to show me your ideas of what you can do with Port... other than drink it."

"Oh, I have been giving it thought, trust me. Much thought."

"Such as?"

"Well, this is simple but effective." He pushed Riley's shirt up and onto his head, blinding him.

"I can't see... aah!"

Roark was swirling one of his nipples with a wine-soaked finger. Then Riley felt Roark's mouth and tongue mimicking the same motion. He grunted. "Now I see..."

Roark pulled away. Riley yanked down his shirt and adjusted the hardness in his pants. "Fuck the sunset, let's just—"

"Ah, patience makes the... libido grow stronger," Roark said and took Riley's hand and led him to the patio. "This sunset is spectacular."

"I bet not as spectacular as you are," Riley rejoined.

They watched the sunset for a few minutes, the sexual tension and anticipation nearly killing Riley. And he knew Roark felt the same, when he finally said, "I'm going to get the other bottle and be right back.

He returned and again took Riley by the hand and led him to the bedroom, saying nothing this time. Riley couldn't ever remember being this disturbed... or horny. Even if he hadn't had sex in a while, this was something different. He knew instinctively that this would be beyond sex. Transcendent. Where had that word come from? But, yes, that's what it would be.

They entered the bedroom and Riley felt his desire crank up a couple of levels. He took their glasses and the newly opened bottle, and set them on the bedside table. He turned to Roark and reached for the buttons of his shirt, fumbling, he undid them as rapidly as his frantic fingers could. He needed to see Roark's bare flesh. He pushed the shirt off and threw it to the floor. He took a step back and stared blatantly. Every nerve in him fired off at the sight of Roark's muscled torso, nearly hairless, only a dusting of light, dark blond hairs on his upper chest and the perfect little "treasure trail" into his waistband. He got an idea. He put his hands on the slab of chest and pushed.

Roark fell back onto the bed and lay... waiting. He put his arms behind his neck. Riley gaped at the flexed biceps, and hoped he wasn't drooling. Fuck, he's gorgeous!

His turn. He pulled his own shirt over his head and let Roark look at him. He saw Roark's eyes darken, and heard his sudden intake of breath. Riley knew he liked what he saw. He kept himself in shape, the gym, running, and never worried about taking his shirt off at the beach. But right now he was glad he looked good for Roark. It was important to him.

Riley picked up a glass and sipped. "Port is definitely my new favorite drink." He licked the rim of the glass slowly, causing a small grunt from Roark. He took another small sip and lowered himself to Roark. He let the Port dribble over Roark's nipple, then he thrust out his tongue and swirled it around the erect nub.

Roark groaned loudly. "You learn fast."

"Good teacher." Riley reached for the glass again and repeated the act with the other nipple.

"You're killing me," Roark muttered.

"Well, then, let's try this." Riley reached for the bottle and poured the dark liquid between Roark's pecs. Then he covered his body with his own. Their wine-and -sweat-soaked torsos slid over one another as Riley's lips found Roark's.

Roark flipped Riley to his back, his mouth descending.

"How did you know to get red sheets?" Riley said, while his neck was being ravaged.

"A dream," Roark said, and bit Riley's earlobe.

"Oh God, I think I'm dying," Riley yelled.

Roark's tongue grew more frantic on Riley's neck and ear, then moved down to his shoulder and biceps. "Not yet. I'm only just starting."

Riley moaned again, louder this time. "Okay, you asked for it." He violently rolled Roark off him and reversed their positions. He leaned above Roark, grabbed both of his arms and pinned them over his head. Riley grinned wickedly. "God, you're hot." He lowered his head to Roark's, lips parted, covering Roark's mouth in a searing, passionate kiss. Their tongues lashed against one another's. *I could kiss this man forever.* But he knew he wanted more from this man. He wanted to experience everything. No limits.

His mouth and tongue explored the column of Roark's neck, tasting the salty flesh, and still tasting the sweetness of the Port. He didn't know which taste made him more light-headed.

He reveled and marveled at the tautness of Roark's flesh, the firm pectorals, the tight abdomen. While not gym-muscled (like himself), Roark had the natural, outdoorsy, masculine muscles. Riley licked and kissed it all. He'd released his hold on Roark's arms, so that he could better explore his body with his hands and fingers. But Roark had kept his arms above his head, periodically flinching or jerking from the ministrations of Riley's expert tongue and hands.

Riley's mission was to taste every square inch of Roark, but he didn't know if he could hold out that long. Every taste and touch of the man was driving him wild. And from Roark's reactions, he could tell he was feeling the same way.

And he hadn't even gotten to the most interesting part yet!

As he moved lower his chest could feel the hardness in Roark's chinos. And from the feel he could tell they were well-matched.

But he had to wait. He wanted to make it last as long as possible. He wanted it to be perfect for Roark.

He unbuttoned the chinos, revealing the large bulge, barely encased in snow-white briefs. *These have to be the tightest whities I've ever seen!* He couldn't resist. He bent and kissed Roark through the white cotton. Roark jerked violently and gave a loud gasp.

Riley raised his eyes and they met Roark's. He let a small smile escape.

Instead of continuing to caress Roark's turgidness, he licked his inner thigh, causing another spasmodic jerk. Then he descended his body, determined to keep his goal of tasting every part.

And he kept his promise, and several minutes later, he wa ready to continue by pushing the even tighter whities down Roark's thighs, letting him spring free at last.

Roark said his first words in quite a while, rasping, "You're torturing me."

Riley smiled wide staring down at the fully naked man. "Yes, I am. But no more." He opened his mouth and took Roark in.

Roark screamed, "Riley!"

An hour—and two orgasms later—Riley lay in Roark's arms, their sweat drying in the warm air. Roark said, "I have been many places and had many astounding experiences, but this past hour may be the most outstanding of them all."

"I know it's mine. I've never felt so comfortable with someone—especially the first time. I've also never tried some of those… things before." He nuzzled Roark's chest. "And I liked it."

"What 'things?' Roark said demurly, all the while kneading the muscles in Riley's upper back.

Riley suddenly felt shy. "You know… like after you… you know… and I… you know…" Riley's head rocked up and down on Roark's chest, the muscles flexing while he laughed.

"Eloquently put, my sexy short-stop. And I do indeed know what you' re referring to."

"Um, I played left field."

"That may be, but the alliteration worked much better with 'sexy short-stop.'

Now Riley was laughing. He bit Roark's nipple.

Roark tried to push his head away, but Riley held firm.

He nibbled some more, then said, "That's for being so smart. Isn't it amazing how easily a simple nipple bite can humble a guy. He bit again, eliciting another grunt from Roark.

"Quite," Roark responded and clutched Riley's head into his chest. What is that adage? If you can't beat 'em, join 'em."

"That's the one," Riley mumbled, moving to the other nipple.

They slept together soundly for a couple of hours, until, abruptly, Riley jumped up out of Roark's arms, yelling, "Roark!"

Roark sat up just as abruptly. "Riley? Riley, what is it? What's the matter?"

"I saw it... us... I... it was so real. The two of us, falling into a... a pit... or room."

Roark pulled Riley into him. "It was a dream, Riley, a dr—" He stopped and pulled back, looking at Riley. Cautiously, he said, "Do you remember anything else? Where you were? What country?"

Riley closed his eyes, thought hard. "Egypt. We were in Egypt." His eyes flew open, puzzled.

"Yes. I have had that dream recently." Roark's voice was flat.

"What does it mean, Roark?"

Roark leaned over and kissed his forehead, murmuring, "I'm not quite sure."

"For the first time in my life, I'm scared. The plane. This dream. Is it a premonition? Do I have what you have? How did I get it? Is this what it feels like when you have these dreams? This is awful. I don't like it. I don't want this." His voice rose on the last statement.

"You mustn't let it worry you. We'll figure this out... together. I won't leave you." Roark looked earnestly into Riley's eyes. "I don't want to leave you. There is something extraordinary happening here. Not only the dreams, our situation..." He swallowed hard. "My feelings..." He smiled warmly. "To use a Rodgers and Hart lyric, *'Bewitched, Bothered, and Bewildered am I.'*"

Riley felt his throat closing, but managed to say, "I like that song. From *Pal Joey*." He gave a small laugh. "I always thought it would be cool to be him—Joey. Well, the gay version."

"I can picture you."

"You said 'feelings.' What do you mean?" He stroked Roark's chest, looking into his eyes.

Roark took his hand and moved it over his heart. "Feelings, my left-fielder." Smiling, he added, "Deep feelings."

Riley felt his eyes fill. "Yeah." he took Roark's hand and put it over his own heart. Then he leaned up, and ever so softly captured Roark's lips with his own, their hands still clasped over one another's hearts.

As they kissed, Riley felt moisture on his cheeks. His?

Roark's? He brought his arms up around Roark's neck and deepened the kiss, feeling the same rush of emotion boomeranging back from Roark. Love? The thought pierced his mind, while he thrilled to the teasing terpsichore of their tongues. Yes. he may very well be falling in love. All his senses were on high alert. His skin prickled with the electricity of every touch and caress.

A supernatural need arose in him, more than the pure physical, almost innate. Not a premonition, but something more primal told him they belonged together.

Hours later, they lay in the dark and Riley whispered, "Egypt. We need to go to Egypt."

The whispered response, "Yes, we do."

They spent the next several days together, packing and preparing for their journey—between their insatiable bouts of lovemaking.

Riley found himself falling more and more in love with Roark, afraid to express his feelings, though, all the while praying that Roark was falling just as hard. He thought so, but no formal words had been said yet.

"Our flight and hotel accommodations are all set, " Roark said, wrapping his arms around Riley from behind and squeezing the pectoral muscles on his naked chest. "I daresay, you are the first man I've met who should never wear a shirt."

"It is summer in Las Vegas." Riley turned around to face Roark, and looked down to admire the manly, muscled chest before him. "I can do you one better, professor. I daresay, you are the first man I've met who should never wear anything." His hands went to Roark's shorts and undid the snap at his waist.

Roark dropped his hands to his sides. "Before you continue your ravishment of my body, did you contact the caretaker for your house in Scottsdale?"

"Yes, all taken care of." He unzipped the shorts. I also called my realtor and put my house on the market."

"You did? Why?" Roark's shorts fell to the floor.

"I don't want it. Or need it." His fingers ran around the waistband of Roark's briefs. "I really never liked it. It's too isolated." His hands slid down inside and encompassed Roark's bare buttocks and squeezed. "And lonely. I might just get a condo somewhere. Maybe here…" His hand came around to the front to grasp Roark's now very hard erection. "In Vegas."

Roark sucked in his breath at the touch. "Here would be a good choice, I think."

Riley continued his fondling with one hand, while deftly sliding Roark's briefs down with his other. He knelt down. "Yes, I like it here."

* * *

"I think you've spoiled me for first class," Riley said, sipping champagne, while holding Roark's hand.

"It was definitely a good idea to spend the night in New York. Although, we didn't exactly get a good night's rest." Roark squeezed Riley's hand.

"It wasn't my fault… really," Riley demurred.

"And whose idea were the Zipties?"

"In my head it sounded like a good idea." Riley shrugged.

"I understand, and it only took a couple of hours for me to regain full circulation."

Riley disengaged his hand and hit Roark in the chest. "It wasn't that long."

Ignoring the blow, Roark continued, "And the ligature marks should fade in a week or two."

"There weren't ligature—"

"Ahem, more champagne?" a male voice said.

Riley felt himself redden, while the flight attendant tipped the bottle to refill his glass. He noticed Roark quietly chuckling. "Not funny."

"On the contrary, watching you blush like that was most amusing."

"Now he'll think I'm some abusive lover or something." He downed the entire flute of champagne in one gulp.

"You are most definitely 'or something,' my sexy lover."

Riley sobered. "Am I? Am I your lover?" He found himself holding his breath waiting for Roark's answer.

Roark stared at him, a warmth coming into his eyes. "How could you doubt it?"

"I… sometimes, you now, I think you're too good to be true. Things happened pretty fast between us. Then we were in New York again, where asshole Chad lives… the plane…"

"Ah yes, how thoughtless of me. I'm sorry."

"No, no, it's all right. After we were together at the hotel, it was fine. I actually forgot all about him, and the plane… well, I think I've got it in something like perspective." He grabbed Roark's hand again. "But I want his—us—to work so bad, I… just… God!… you've overwhelmed me. You haven't done anything to make me doubt you. I mean, you're perfect. I guess it's me; I don't trust it— trust myself—enough." He stopped and nodded several times. "Yeah, that's it. It's not you; it's me. I do trust you, Roark. Now I need to trust me as well." He swallowed hard. "I… I love you." He snapped his eyes shut. "Shit. Fuck. I'm sorry. I swore I wasn't gonna say it. It just came out."

He turned as best he could in the seat, angling himself to face Roark. "No. Fuck it. I don't care. I love you. If you don't like it, that's on you. I'm not a game player. That was Chad, never telling me anything. I'm not gonna do it anymore. Life's too short. I'm too old for this shit. I love you and that's it." He nodded hard once again, more to himself than Roark. "I need more champagne, my rant made me thirsty."

Miraculously, the flight attendant was there and refilling. "Thank you," Riley said, and took a big sip.

The plane hit a bump.

Riley's glass rocked in his hand. The glass slipped from his mouth and emptied down the front of his white polo shirt, covering it.

"Fuck!" Riley shouted, way louder than he knew he should have.

The flight attendant was back instantly. "Are you all right, Mr. Miller?" Then, noticing Riley's soaked shirt, dashed away and returned in a moment with a cloth for Riley to dry with.

"Thank you," Riley said, and began to blot and rub at his chest. "I've got a T-shirt in my carry-on."

The flight attendant, whose name tag said "Blake," volunteered, "I'll get it for you." He reached up into the overhead bin. "The green one?"

"Yeah, that's it." Riley said handing his glass to the silent Roark. He tugged his soaked shirt off over his head.

Thud.

"Oh, I'm so sorry!" Blake said, retrieving Riley's bag from the floor where he had accidentally dropped it.

Roark spoke, "Quite all right, Blake. There's nothing breakable in there." He passed the bag to the bare-chested Riley. "I feel the same way everytime Riley takes his shirt off as well."

If Blake had been naked, Riley was sure he could have seen the flummoxed flight attendant blush to his toes.

Blake stuttered, "Ril—M-M-Mr. Miller, I'm so sorry…"

"It's okay, Blake," Riley assured the still red-faced man. He retrieved the green T-shirt from his bag and zipped it up.

Roark took the bag and handed it to Blake, who carefully returned it to the overhead.

Riley donned his shirt, and Roark took the wet polo and held it out to Blake. "If you would be so good as to dispose of this please, Blake?" Blake took it, and Roark said, "Or keep it a souvenir." He added a quick smile.

Blake turned scarlet again. "Could I? Thank you. Thank you so much. He clutched the wet shirt to his chest and scurried away.

"Yuck," Riley said. "It's all wet and smells—"

"Like you," Roark finished. "I'm sure it will be his most treasured possession, since he obviously recognized you. He'll bring it out at parties and show it off—I'm sure with an elaborately embellished story."

"Stop, you're going to make me throw up my nuts."

Roark gave smirk.

"The peanuts, pervert."

Blake returned with the bottle of champagne and a new glass, his shirt a bit damp. "Try again? The pilot said we shouldn't have any more turbulence. And he apologizes to you." He leaned over and said conspiratorially, "He's a big fan."

Riley took the new glass from Blake. "Thank you. And thank the pilot too. He's doing a great job. It's not his fault. And if you'll get his address and also yours I'll send you both autographed baseballs."

Blake's mouth dropped open. "Oh-My-God! Really? Yes! Yes, of course I'll get you the addresses away!" He thrust out the bottle. "Here take the whole thing." he shoved the bottle at Riley and ran off.

Riley took a sip… then…

"Here you are, Riley... Riley's okay isn't it? I can call you Mr. Miller—"

"Riley's good," Riley said.

"Great! Thank you. Here are the addresses." Then he handed another piece of paper to Riley. "Here's my phone number too... in case... in case you need anything. Thank you. Thank you again."

"Well, this should tide us over for awhile," Roark said. He held his glass out for Riley to refill it. He obliged. "Thank you. It appears that when you are a famous, good-looking athlete people (literally) fall all over themselves to help you and ply you with liquor. Do you ever have to pay for your drinks?" Roark was dead-pan.

Riley set the bottle on the floor between his legs. "Sometimes," Riley said, refusing to take the bait. "But not often." He sipped, giving Roark a "get used to it" look. Then he sobered, "And about what I said before..."

"Yes about that..." Roark joined in. "You need not be ashamed or concerned about sharing your feelings with me. I am not a 'game-player' either. I believe in total honesty."

"But I—"

Roark continued, speaking over Riley. "I love you too."

Riley's mouth dropped open. "What? You do? How? I'm just the dumb baseball—ex-baseball—player. And you're handsome and rich, super-intelligent..."

"Riley, please. You are selling yourself far too short. You, my friend... my love, have more heart and caring inside you than any ten men I've met. As well as being intelligent in your own right." He put his hand over Riley's. "I don't see how I couldn't have fallen in love with you."

Riley felt his throat tighten. "Did you see this? Dream about this? Us, together?"

"No, I haven't had any visions or precognitive dreams since I met you."

Under his breath, Riley said, "Shit."

"Riley?"

"I have," Riley muttered.

"Have... ?"

"Had dreams. More than that nightmare at your place. No dream where you said you loved me, but I've seen us together. On the plane. Here. Now. You in your dove-gray button down, me in a green T-shirt, drinking champagne. They're usually just bits and pieces, not full scenes. Like, I didn't see me spill the champagne. I saw us in New York, and I saw us in Egypt. Or see us in Egypt. It's so weird. Sphinx, pyramids, the whole nine yards." He stopped and took a drink, feeling better that he'd told Roark everything. And even better because he knew that Roark loved him. Him! Incredible. Then he said, "Really?"

Roark's eyes focused on him with a question in them.

"Really, you love me?" he still couldn't believe his luck.

Roark's eyes warmed with love and he smiled. "Yes, Riley. Don't doubt it... or yourself."

Riley wa so caught up with emotion he couldn't speak.

Roark rescued him. "How about some more of that

champagne and we'll toast our future?"

Riley refilled their glasses.

Their eyes met, glasses raised. Roark said, "Dreams or no dreams, we will make our future." Clink.

"My turn," Riley said, raising his glass again. "This is to you. Even before I had any kind of vision, I knew that when I met you, my life would change—had changed—and that something extraordinary was going to happen. My life was at a turning point, waiting. Waiting for something, or someone, to take me to the next phase of my life. You're that someone. And falling in love with you, is that something." He clinked his glass to Roark's. "My Roark."

Riley watched one tiny tear at the corner of Roark's eye glisten and trickle down his cheek.

Yes, this was love. Riley knew it deep in his soul. It was as if this is what his life had been leading up to—what he had been waiting for. The feeling of deja vu came over him. But he knew he'd never been here or felt like this before. Still…

They continued talking and drinking, Riley now feeling a great calm and security knowing Roark loved him. They both finally fell asleep for the rest of the flight—drunk on champagne and love.

They landed in Cairo, and after retrieving their luggage, hailed a taxi to their hotel. The heat in the city seemed to have a different oppressiveness than that in Las Vegas. More arid. Stultifying.

"I thought Vegas was hot," Riley said. "The hotel's air-conditioned, right?"

"Of course," Roark said, then turned to the driver, saying

something in Arabic.

"I'm not surprised," Riley said, "but it's cool that you can speak Arabic. I like the sound of it. Would you teach me?"

"'Aywa." Roark smiled.

"I hope that was 'yes.'"

"It was. I would be happy to teach you." Roark lowered his voice so the driver couldn't hear. "Let's start with, 'ana bahibbak.'"

"I like that," Riley said. "Does it mean what I think?"

Roark nodded, the warmth in his eyes conveying the meaning of the words.

"Then 'ana bahibbak too," Riley whispered back, then leaned in to kiss him.

Roark put up a hand. "Remember where you are. We cannot be as carefree here as in other countries."

"Oh yeah, right. Forgot." He added, "But then, I forget a lot of things around you." He gave a wide grin. "Duly chastened, Professor. I'll keep my hands... and lips off—at least until I get you alone. Then all bets are off."

Roark drew in a deep breath and his eyes darkened. "We're almost at the hotel."

"Good. I think I'll just make it then. It's been almost a whole day since I've had you."

"I'm well aware."

Riley could see Roark's desire matched his own.

A couple of hours later they'd settled in their hotel, and they lay in each other's arms, completely sated.

Roark wiped at the sweat on Riley's smooth chest, saying, "I believe I have discovered Eden here in Egypt."

"You can be Eve then. And I'll be the serpent who tempts her." He traced his tongue over Roark's neck until he elicited the gasp/groan he was waiting for.

"You're killing me," Roark murmured. "But at least I'll die a happy man."

It was another half hour before either spoke.

"I need food," Riley declared. "You wore me out—something I thought I would never say."

"It, in truth, is something I always hoped I would say. I believe you hit a home run, Mr. Baseball Player. So, I thank you."

"My pleasure I hope I covered all the bases." Riley couldn't resist the baseball double entendre. "Now. Food." He gave Roark a lingering kiss, then sprang up abruptly. "Let's go."

They ate a local restaurant, mere yards from the hotel.

"This lamb, whatever, is great," Riley said, swallowing, "But I was so hungry, I probably could have eaten it raw."

"I'm glad you enjoyed the tagine, Egyptians primarily eat beef, but they do prepare some excellent lamb and mutton dishes as well."

"Are these prunes? I like the sweetness with the rice and the, I think, it's squash or pumpkin maybe."

"Correct on all three. That's why it is a favorite of mine, the combining of the different tastes and textures."

"You've been here before, right?" Riley said, finishing his last bite of tagine.

"Yes, but Cairo only."

"What do you mean? You haven't been to Karnak or the City of the Dead—Saqqara?"

"Strangely, no."

Riley saw an anomalous look come over Roark's rugged face, a questioning, intense look. He suddenly felt uneasy, scared. "Roark, what is it?"

Then as if nothing had transpired in him, Roark's face brightened. "I think we should go there." He looked off into the distance, his eyes not seeming to focus on anything. "We need to go there."

Riley had the sense that Roark's last statement was spoken to himself. His uneasiness grew. "Naw, it's all right; we don't have to. I'm good here. I mean, we've got the Great Pyramid, the Sphinx—"

"No," Roark said. A little vehemently, Riley thought. "Nonsense. We have the time. We will go there. The Sphinx can wait." Roark forced a smile, his tone became carefree. "She's been there for centuries; she's not going anywhere. We'll leave tomorrow morning. It's a mere forty kilometers, twenty-five miles. Would you like to take a dromedary?"

"A camel? I'll pass." He winked at Roark, hoping to alleviate the tension he'd felt had arisen. "I don't want to bruise my ass on the hump. I might need it for other things."

"A taxi it is,' Roark rejoined. "We wouldn't want to bruise anything so valuable… or perfect."

Riley smiled, everything ostensibly back to normal. "Thanks. I—and my perfect ass—appreciate it." The mood, though, had changed, and Riley, normally a dessert fiend, found himself not hungry anymore. "I think I'm stuffed, and beat. The jet lag—and the physical activity—have done me in. If we're going to be trekking across the desert, let's eschew dessert."

"Very witty, my friend. But I insist we try the Umm ali: phyllo pastry, cream, nuts, raisins, coconut flakes…"

"Sold. It sounds incredible. Anything with coconut, and I'm in. I'll make room for it."

"The Egyptians usually have fruit for dessert, but they do have some delicious desserts in their own right. This is one of the most popular."

Riley felt they were just about back to normal. Dessert would help.

That night Riley dreamed.

Sand everywhere. Ten or more statues lined an enormous wall. They loomed over him, several stories high.

Pyramids, hundreds of them—or so it seemed. All sizes. Short. Tall.

Cats. Carved on the walls. Frozen. Waiting.

Colorful scenes on stone: men force-feeding geese, cattle crossing a canal, scores of men dragging a sled with an enormous statue.

Coffins. Sarcophagi. Mummies.

Gold. Jewels. Urns of alabaster.

Riley flowed through them all, as if he himself were being drawn across the desert sands on his own sled. He couldn't move or resist.

A monolithic pyramid loomed before him. He was inexorably drawn to it. A passage appeared in the side of it and he flowed in.

He was in a tomb. He knew it.

Then… darkness.

He was inside the pyramid. The tomb. He could smell the staleness. The acrid dryness. The pungent smell of death.

He was still moving—floating.

A dim light appeared, growing brighter.

He was in a large chamber. Two stone slabs lay before him; atop them the effigaic statues of those buried beneath.

The walls depicted hieroglyphic symbols and pulchritudinous painted images, vividly depicting battles and ceremonies to the deities.

At the heads of each of the sarcophagi, on a columned decorated pedestal, sat a canopic jar, luridly painted in florid colors and encrusted with gems of varying sizes.

The tomb was lit by wall sconces, casting an eerie light throughout.

The floor began to shake.

The jars moved.

Riley felt himself move, no longer being drawn along. He could feel ground beneath him. And that ground began to move. The shaking grew more powerful. He could feel himself falling.

Darkness again.

He screamed.

Then arms were around him, holding him tightly.

"Riley! Riley, my love, my love! I'm here. You're all right."

Roark.

He opened his eyes and met Roark's emerald ones. He saw the concern and fear there. His panting began to slow. His nude body was covered in sweat—and it was cold. He began to shiver. Roark pulled the sheet up over his upper body and tried to rub warmth into him.

"Can you talk? Do you want to tell me about it?" Roark said, planting a light kiss on Riley's forehead,

Riley felt Roark's body heat beginning to warm him, assuring him. "I… He hesitated, not sure why he didn't want to tell Roark. He should understand. He's had the same freaky dreams. Maybe he can help me.

"I have stopped dreaming since we… since our first time together. It's as if the dreaming has transferred to you. I would not have wished that for you. I know how disconcerting they can be." Roark pulled Riley closer.

Riley closed his eyes and hugged back, feeling the calm and warmth, trying not to think. 'We… I… I'm not sure you were there. I didn't see you. But I felt you… your presence. We were in a tomb, I think, I thought it was a cave at first. Now I think it was a vault—a pyramid vault. There were two sarcophagi. The room was lit, and the walls were painted brilliantly. Hieroglyphics, scenes of battles,

Egyptian gods… Then there was a rumbling, like an earthquake. The ground shook. Then it was all blackness. I fell… I screamed… Then I woke up. That's all I can remember. No. No… there were these two jars or urns, maybe, one at the head of each sarcophagus."

"Canopic jars," Roark said grimly.

"Yeah, I guess. You know about them? Have you been there?"

"No, I haven't. But they were very common in crypts of the royalty. They could contain various things: jewelry, precious items, even the internal organs from the embalming."

"Yick, if we find any, remind me not to open them. The smell would probably kill me. Oh, and these canopic-urn things had jewels all over them."

"Then they were undoubtedly Royals. Perhaps you saw a pharaoh and his wife or son. If this indeed a prescient vision, Riley, maybe you will discover a hidden tomb."

"Uh, I'd rather not. It didn't give me a warm and fuzzy feeling. But I wish I hadn't woken up so soon. I want to know what happened next."

"Your next dream, perhaps?"

"So, you think there'll be more?"

"Who knows? Yours seem to be frequent enough. Mine were always sporadic. I never had any warning. They were always spontaneous."

"Do you think that means something?"

"Again, I can't say. My conjecture would be yes. There is

something happening here—between us. About us."

"Well, I hope it's good."

Roark smiled at him, his eyes warming. "I cannot imagine anything but good where you're concerned. You have a beautiful soul and spirit, alive and loving." He leaned over a kissed Riley deeply.

"Thank you for your faith in me, "Riley said, licking his lips and savoring the kiss. "I feel the same about you. And deep, deep, inside, I know we were meant to find each other."

"I know that as well. You are also my 'dream man,' if you'll pardon the pun."

Riley laughed. 'I love it. 'Dream man.' Like that old song. 'You Stepped Out of a Dream."

"Dream Lover."

"Dream a Little Dream of Me."

"A Dream Is a Wish Your Heart Makes."

"Cinderella, right?" Riley said.

"Yes."

Riley raised his eyebrow wryly. "Just so long as it isn't "The Impossible Dream."

"It couldn't be." Roark swallowed hard. "I had thought it impossible to find anyone as perfect as you are; Riley Miller—baseball star"

Now Riley found his own throat closing. There was so much he wanted to say, but didn't. There would be time. Forever, he hoped. Instead of responding, he pulled Roark to him and conveyed his thoughts, hopes, love and dreams in a long blistering kiss.

Roark blinked hard as he finally withdrew. "My... Thank you, Riley. You have made the impossible possible."

"Cinderella again? Only the musical this time."

Roark laughed hard. "You like musicals, I take it."

"Love 'em. Hey, I'm gay right? Comes with the territory."

Roark laughed louder and they fell back on the bed together, making their wishes come true.

"How about some Egyptian coffee to jump-start our day, and to bolster us for our trek across the desert?" Roark asked Riley as he donned his white camp-shorts.

Riley popped his head through the neck of his T-shirt. "Sounds good. It's kind of thick isn't it?"

"Yes, it's made similarly to Turkish coffee; grounds, water and sugar are brought to a boil several times, hence the thickness."

"I've never had it. You like it?"

"I have grown to."

"Okay, let's do it. Then onto the City of the Dead." He put his arm around Roark's shoulders and led him from the room.

Riley found he liked Egyptian coffee, and after his third cup declared, "If I have one more cup, I'm going to be able to fly us there. I'm wired enough to light up Cairo for a week."

"I think 'wired' is an apt term for you. I believe we have enough water and supplies for our arid foray."

They gathered their backpacks and exited the hotel.

"You know, in the light of day—and three cups of the strongest coffee I've ever had—I think I'm feeling better about all this. Like it's going to turn out all right," Riley said after they'd been on the road for awhile.

"Did you dream again after we fell back asleep?" Roark probed.

"I did, but it was different, more surreal than real. We were flying—like on a magic carpet flying. We were dressed like sheikhs or something. But it didn't seem like now. If it was the future, that would be weird. I mean, how could that be? I thought these dream-vision things showed the future?"

"I wish I could help, Riley. But this a phenomenon. There are no rules or answers that I know of."

"But a magic flying carpet? Come on."

"I'm only speculating, but perhaps it's a metaphorical vision. As I said, no rules."

Riley lowered his voice, not wanting the driver to hear. "I want more than anything for my vision to be literally true. I want to fly off into the sunset on a magic carpet with you."

Roark, smiling, said, "My fervent wish as well, and to paraphrase a familiar quote, 'There are stranger things in Heaven and Earth, Riley...'"

"So it seems. I mean, beyond the... weird stuff, I never thought I would be driving through the hot Egyptian desert headed to Saqqara, the City of the Dead," again lowering his voice, finished, "with my very own hot, Indiana Jones-type adventurer. You even wore his hat." He flicked the brim of Roark's hat. "Where'd you get it? I meant to ask you before when you put it on in the room, but then when you... uh..." He looked at the driver. "Uh, kissed me, I forgot."

"So sorry for the distraction. I will endeavor not to do so again if it affects you so terribly."

Riley squinted hard at Roark. "You'd better not not distract me. As a matter of fact, I want you to distract me like that, as often as possible." His point made, he continued, "So, where did you get the Indy hat?"

"I am a little embarrassed, but I bought it in Australia several years ago, after the release of *Indiana Jones and the Crystal Skull*, the fourth movie, or third sequel. And with my gallivanting around the world, I decided I wanted an 'adventuring' hat. It's silly I know... but there you have it. You are the only person I have ever told that to, and if you reveal my secret to anyone else, I will not be held accountable for my actions."

Riley was laughing hard during Roark's tirade and when he finally got himself together, said, "That was so British upper-crusty... pompous, but... cool. How did you learn to do that? And by the way, you're really cute when you blush."

And in response, Roark blushed again. "I guess I did sound rather priggish, didn't I?"

Riley affected his best British, drawing out the first syllable as much as he could. "Raaaaww-ther." He punched Roark in the chest after he said it. "But I like it. You're this anachronism of British-

American, smart-guy, hot-guy, book-guy, sex-guy. It's awesome."

"I'm glad you approve." And Riley watched Roark's third blush.

"I just hope you don't bust a blood vessel in your head with all that blushing you're doing." Riley lightly patted him on the cheek.

And, for a fourth time, Roark reddened.

Riley opened his mouth to comment again—and froze, mouth agape, his eyes fixed forward.

After they'd initially left Cairo, Riley had noted the Nile, the people, the desert around them, but afterward had remained focused on Roark. Now what he saw in front of him had him gazing in wonderment.

Saqqara: The City of the Dead. The enormous stone edifices stood imposingly before them. Roark followed Riley's gaze and had a similar reaction.

The taxi stopped.

"I have seen photos… the Pyramids, but they do not do justice to this magnificence." Roark said.

They got out of the taxi and Roark paid the driver. They retrieved their backpacks from the trunk and walked toward the towering wall in front of them. The brick face soared two hundred feet or more into the air. The facade was covered with gargantuan statues of gods and pharaohs.

Tourists abounded, photographing the vast—there was no other word for it—edifice.

"Incredible," Riley said, at last finding his voice.

"Indubitably," Roark added.

"I would have thought you would have seen things like this before, among your travels," Riley said.

"That is the beauty of traveling. I am always in awe of what man can create. What we would think would be impossible, given the time period and logistical constraints, they somehow managed to overcome and achieve. I am never not in awe of man's miracles."

Riley nodded. "I can see that. I mean, I think the Statue of Liberty and the Empire State Building, or even the glitzy casinos in Vegas are all pretty impressive on their own."

"Exactly, my adventurous sidekick. I am in awe of their constructions as well, the architecture and engineering are truly mind-blowing." Roark extended an arm toward the passage between two monolithic statues. "Shall we?"

They walked for a bit, marveling, barely noticing the extreme heat. "Riley, make sure to keep hydrated," Roark admonished. "This is a dry heat, like Las Vegas, and dehydration can sneak up on you, and before you know it: heat exhaustion—or worse. It's quite common." And to make his point he took a long draught from his water bottle. Riley followed suit.

"Yes, Professor-slash-doctor." He took another swig, then abruptly said. "Let's go."

"Do you want to see the pharaoh Djoser's complex in the middle over there? That is the most famous structure in Saqqara, one I have longed to explore. Djoser's personal architect, Imhotep, constructed it. It is said to be the first pyramid in Egypt."

"I…" Riley hesitated, then relented, wanting to please Roark. "Sure, let's see it."

There were quite a few people gathered around the outside of the large pyramid taking photos and admiring. At the entrance was a small group of twelve or so who all appeared to be American. A dark complected man with black hair and moustache was speaking in Arabic-inflected English to them. "The Step Pyramid of the pharaoh Djoser is the first step pyramid ever built by the renowned architect Imhotep between 2630 and 2611 BC. Before this, pharaohs were buried in stone mustabas—the one level flat structures you see here in Saqqara. Imhotep created this pyramid by building one mustaba on top of the other in decreasing sizes creating the 'steps.' Around the city you will see other structures by Imhotep built for his pharaoh Djoser. The actual burial chamber of Djoser is said to be in an underground chamber of the pyramid. Its whereabouts have as yet to be discovered, as well the burial place of Imhotep.

"Imhotep was often confused with the god, Thoth, the god of architecture, mathematics and medicine. Imhotep was also the patron of scribes and several statues of him have been found showing him with papyrus scrolls. It is also said that there is a legend ascribed to him that he ended a seven-year famine during Djoser's reign through a dream he had in which the Nile god Khnum spoke to him, promising to end the drought."

The crowd around was completely silent, totally enrapt in the mythology of Egypt.

"Much mystery surrounds Imhotep, and that is why his name

and legend have been used in your American television shows and films, the most popular being *The Mummy* and its sequels."

There were many nods from the tourists who had obviously seen the films.

"The reign of Djoser and his Vizier, Imhotep, is decidedly the most revered era in Egyptian history," the guide concluded.

The group began chatting among themselves as they moved off to their next destination. Riley and Roark remained behind.

Riley said, "I remember in *The Mummy* movie the hordes of people all chanting 'Im-ho-tep, Im-ho-tep.' It was eerie. I love that movie."

"Yes, I enjoyed it as well. The mummy concept has always fascinated people, especially Americans. They are one of the oldest civilizations and mystery has always surrounded them. Add to that the fact that Imhotep's tomb has never been discovered only enhances the mystique."

"And they've never found Djoser's tomb either, right?"

"Correct."

"But it's supposed to be here." Riley had an idea. "We can go inside, can't we?

"Yes, why?"

"I have a feeling… part of my dream. I'm supposed to go inside…"

"But your dream had you screaming. The earthquake…"

"I know, but I have to find out what it meant. It's important. Please, Roark." Riley realized he was pleading, out of character for him. "Look the tour group is going inside. Let's go with them."

"If you're sure. Whatever you want."

"Thank you, Roark. Thank you." This wasn't like him. What was he doing? He'd never been an obsessive person—not even in his desire to win the World Series. Sure, he'd wanted to win; he'd wanted to win more than anything. He loved baseball; it was his passion. But he hadn't been obsessed. Now, he was. In truth, he admitted inwardly, he felt possessed.

He needed to calm down. Think for a moment. Roark. He needed Roark. His sensibility. His rationale.

"Roark. Talk to me."

"Riley, what is it?"

"I don't know. Something's happening to me."

"Do you need water? Do you need to sit down? Is it the heat?" Genuine concern was in his voice and eyes.

"No, physically I feel fine. It's… it's a need. Like a burning… craving… We have to go inside." Riley realized they had already joined the group of tourists. He lowered his voice. "I'm sorry, Roark. Help me."

"I will."

They entered the pyramid. The change from the brilliant sun to the the dimly lit chamber was startling.

Roark held Riley back from the group. "Wait here. Let your eyes adjust. Breathe. His hand held Riley's biceps firmly, comforting. "Deep, slow breaths."

Riley breathed in. He inhaled the cool, musty air of the

pyramid chamber. He tried to focus, concentrate. The tour guide was off ahead to the right speaking to his group. He couldn't make out what was being said. The group was only a few yards away, but to Riley they looked like an amorphous mass way off in the distance. The area seemed vast, but he rationalized it couldn't be; it was just his skewed perception. What was going on with him?

He blinked several times, trying to right his vision. The slow breaths and blinking seemed to help. He felt himself calming down. The gray mass in front of him deformed into individual people. He let out a long breath. He could now feel the warmth of Roark's hand on his arm, slightly kneading.

"Thanks. I'm starting to feel better now." He put one hand on Roark's kneading one and squeezed. "I'm sorry."

"No need. I confess, I feel that there is something unusual happening here as well. Not as intensely as you do. There almost seems to be a presence, a manifestation... It's difficult to be specific. Do you want to continue?"

"Yes," Riley said too quickly. "I mean... Yes, let's continue. I'm fine, now. Really. I'm good."

"As you wish. Follow the crowd?"

Riley's eyes unfocused. He rotated his head to the left. "That way."

"I'm not sure we can go that way. It's dark. There seems to be only wall—"

"No," Riley cut him off. "There's a passage." And he began walking left into the dark.

Roark followed, and several yards later they did, indeed, come to a stone wall.

Roark pulled a flashlight from his pack and scanned the 10x10 foot wall in front of them.

Riley automatically bent down and pushed a crevice at the bottom corner in front of him, and with his other hand pushed a stone further up.

Nothing happened.

Then… the sound of stone grinding on stone. A crack appeared in the side of the wall and a five-foot slab began to recede from the rest of the wall. Roark's light followed the movement until an opening large enough for a small person or child was revealed.

"How did you know, Riley?' Roark voice held a hint of awe.

"I don't know." Riley's eyes had regained their focus, and he acted surprised. "I think, I guess… I just had an out-of-body experience." He lowered his voice to a mere murmur. "Or like I was possessed." His volume increased. "Roark what's happening?" He couldn't stop his desperation. He grabbed Roark's arm.

"I'm not certain. I am as baffled as you. It appears as if we are being guided by something. I also feel drawn to this place. We have to continue, Riley. We are meant to be here. Now. At this moment in time. It's—"

"Our destiny," Riley finished. Yes, I feel it too—guided. But isn't this unexplored? Nobody's ever discovered this, have they?"

"I don't believe so. There are hundreds of hidden chambers in the pyramids here and in Giza. Archaeologists are periodically discovering new ones. Imhotep, the architect of this pyramid and others, was well known for doing this."

"Imhotep," Riley muttered, his voice once again taking on an ethereal tone, unlike the chanting tone he used before when they were talking about the movie. This was a whispered word of reverence. He didn't know why he said it like that, but he seemed helpless to resist. Ineluctable. Kismet. "Roark." He touched Roark's forearm. "I'm scared."

Roark took Riley's hand in both of his. "I'm here for you... always."

Riley snatched his hand back and reached out and pulled Roark into him, their bodies slamming. Roark nearly dropped his flashlight. "Do you mean that? Roark, I need to know."

Roark pulled back to look at him. He shined the light up between them. "I have never meant anything more strongly in my life. I love you."

Riley let out the breath he hadn't realized he'd been holding. He felt his eyes burn. In the eerie shadows from Roark's flashlight, he looked into Roark's eyes. He could actually feel his love, as if it were tangible. "You do. I'm who you've been waiting for. Me. Your soulmate. I knew it! From that moment you sat next to me in the airport and I looked into your emerald-green eyes, I knew it. If you had asked me to go away with you to Timbuktu, I would have. There was something about you I could instinctively trust, like I'd known you forever. Then, when we made love... I knew you were the only man for me. Ever!" He pulled Roark in again, glancing around to make sure the tour group was long gone, and kissed him, long and hard.

Riley pulled back, the light shining between them again. "I love you, Roark." he noted the love reflected in Roark's eyes. "Now I'm not scared. Let's go exploring where, almost, no man has gone before. I mean, it's pretty cool that no one has been here for a couple of thousand years."

"It's very cool, Riley. And it's even cooler that you love me as I do you. This is where we're meant to be."

Riley opened his mouth to speak.

"And," Roark continued, "this was a vision I had. Not recently. A long time ago. I'd almost forgotten it. Most of my visions materialize as reality shortly after I have them. I had written that one off as a normal dream." He smiled. "My dream man."

Riley felt the heat on his face. "Back at you, but I think you're more of a fantasy for me. I never could've dreamed up someone as perfect as you." He laughed. "Jeez, I sound like a bad romance novel—which is my guilty pleasure—romance novels: straight, gay, anything, I love 'em. And now I'm in one! How great is that?"

"Exceptionally great, my love. Shall we venture on?"

"Lay on, Macduff. I told you I would go anywhere with you, anytime."

"I think we'll both need our flashlights." Riley withdrew his from his pack, clicked it on.

They had taken but ten steps, when they heard the crunch again of stone on stone as the hidden wall shut behind them.

"I'm just gonna assume there's another secret thingy on this side of the wall as well to let us out. Right, Roark?"

"There must be. The builders would have needed a way out. Unless, of course, Imhotep didn't want anyone to know of the hidden chamber and made sure the workers were walled in."

"You're kidding, right?" Riley's breathing increased and the musty smell grew stronger. 'That's barbaric."

"It would depend on Imhotep's plans and Pharaoh Djoser's wishes."

"So we might be stuck in here?"

"If it helps, it was not in my vision, as I remember it."

"Well, too late now. Let's keep going."

They walked along the corridor in silence for a few minutes. Riley flipped his flashlight back and forth. The corridor was surprisingly wide, ten or twelve feet, he guessed, and about seven feet high. He stuck out a hand. The walls were smooth, as was the floor, with no markings of any kind.

"I don't know why I keep expecting something… or someone to pop out. Too many 'Mummy' movies, I guess. I need to cut back. It's so quiet…"

"Like a tomb?" Roark interjected.

"Cute." Riley stopped walking. "Roark?"

"Yes?"

"You know what I want to do?"

"I think I might have a good idea."

"We probably shouldn't though."

"The floor is hard. I don't have a blanket or anything to lay down."

"Yeah, well, the floor isn't the only thing that's hard." Riley grabbed Roark's free hand and pulled it to his crotch to prove his point.

Roark squeezed and pulled Riley into him for a hungry kiss. "What if we walk a little further and see if there is a more conducive, or at least somewhat more comfortable area?"

"You sure? It's not like we're going to find a couch. Being alone with you in this dark, creepy, overblown crypt is a turn-on."

Roark released his grip and took a step back. He set his flashlight down, but left it on, casting eerie shadows on the wall. He dropped his backpack, then reached over and took Riley's flashlight from him and set it on the ground, producing more distorted shadows on the opposite wall. He pushed Riley's backpack off his shoulders and set it down as well.

"I—" Riley started.

Roark's lips covered his mouth. His hands slid down Riley's torso and up under his T-shirt. He pushed it up and over his head; their lips briefly parting. His hands moved to Riley's waist. He undid the belt and snap and slid his shorts and underwear down over his hips, setting him free.

Roark stepped back to stare at the naked man. The light from the dual flashlights cast odd shadows and planes on the muscled body. Riley was breathing hard with anticipated lust.

Roark's eyes trailed slowly up his body until they met Riley's.

He pulled his own T-shirt over his head and dropped it to the floor.

Riley's breathing increased.

Roark put his hands to his waistband, undid the button, then unzipped his shorts. He slid them down, leaving on his, now, too tight briefs.

Riley stared… and stared. His mouth was suddenly dry. He licked his lips and swallowed hard. He couldn't recall ever being so turned on or feeling such desire. This was the most exquisite man he'd ever seen; hard, rugged—sexy beyond words. And his. All his. He wanted to take a picture of him, but realized that this image would be forever branded on his memory.

He held his breath as Roark put his fingers in the waistband of his briefs, and inch by agonizing inch revealed himself fully to him. It was if Riley were seeing Roark naked for the first time. Magnificent.

Roark broke the silence. "Help yourself, my love." He held his hands wide away from his body in offering.

Riley closed the gap between them and for the next few minutes the men lost themselves in each other: body, mind and soul. The indescribable feeling of being one.

"I thought the floor would be hard," Riley said, cradling Roark's head to his chest as they held each other in their passionate aftermath.

Roark wiggled his hips into Riley's. "It is odd. I didn't notice any discomfort at all." He rubbed Riley's sweaty chest.

Riley gave a grunt as Roark pinched his nipple. "Note to self:

tomb floors are great for making love."

"I'm not sure I would make it a habit."

"Hey, you don't think we've angered the gods or anything, you know desecrating the tomb, do you?"

"Now you're worried about incurring their wrath?"

"Well, I don't want some mummy's curse thing on us for defiling their sacred burial chamber."

"Only in the movies, Riley."

"If you're sure? I guess we should get up, except I know that both of my arms are completely numb—and I think my ass is too."

"I fear the same. The stone is not forgiving, now that reality has set in."

The men rose slowly, rubbing at their various aches and shaking out their stiff limbs, then dressed.

"I have extra batteries, so we needn't worry on that account, which is why I left them on," Roark said. "The way the lights played off your body was erotically appealing."

"You too, professor. Especially off your bare ass. He slapped Roark on the butt then ran off forward and around a corner.

"Holy shit!" Riley stopped cold. "Roark! Come here!"

Roark hustled around the corner. His mouth dropped open.

"Do you see it? Up ahead?"

There was a faint glow, seeming to come from around a corner at the end of the corridor up ahead.

"What is it, Roark?" Riley was whispering.

"I have no idea. It's not possible. There should be no light in here. I…" He couldn't seem to finish his statement.

"Do you have a gun?" Riley couldn't keep the trepidation from his voice.

"A knife."

"Shit. What do we do? We can't go back. Wait." He grabbed Roark's arm. "I'm getting a feeling… from my dream, I think. I don't remember walking along this corridor… but this might be that chamber up ahead." He pulled at Roark. "I bet it is. We have to see."

He held onto Roark while they walked in silence down the long corridor, the light getting brighter as they neared the end.

They turned the corner.

There it was: the chamber from his dream. Riley gaped in wonder. Fire-lit wall sconces were mounted around the room. In the center, two six-foot-long sarcophagi lay side by side, coptic jars on pedestals at their heads. The floor of the chamber, where the sarcophagi were, was recessed. Four stone steps led down to them.

"This is it, Roark. My dream."

"Yes, I have seen this too." Roark's voice was reverential.

"How can there be fires on these wall sconces?" Who lit them? How long have they been here?" Riley started to get panicky as the thought was finally striking home that his dream was reality.

"I do not know. Of course, it shouldn't be possible, but there is the proof. Perpetual fire."

"It's like magic."

"Magic, yes. That is as good an answer as any."

Riley turned to look at Roark. Roark's eyes were transfixed.

"Roark, are you all right? You're scaring me."

Roark began to mumble.

Riley couldn't understand the words. He thought they might be Egyptian. "What? What are you saying? Roark? Roark!"

The fires on the walls flickered, as if a strong breeze had just come up. Except Riley felt no breeze. The air was as still as… a tomb.

Roark continued his litany.

The flames continued to flicker.

The ground began to shake.

The walls moved.

An earthquake, Riley thought.

His dream.

The ground shook more forcefully.

The fires went out.

A violent tremor.

Riley felt the floor give way. The room was black. He screamed, "Roark!" as he fell, clutching at empty air. His head struck something, and he thought he heard Roark's voice invoke, "Djoser!" as he blacked out.

Riley woke, rubbing the back of his head. There was light. He was laying on the floor of the burial chamber. The sconces were all lit. He rose slowly. "Roark? Roark?" Where was he? He looked around, not seeing him.

There. On the floor on the other side of the now-opened? sarcophagus, he saw two legs sticking out. He rushed over.

Roark lay there, silent—unmoving. Riley knelt down and raised his head gently. "Roark? Roark, please wake up."

Nothing.

He put his head to Roark's chest. He could hear a heartbeat. Thank God. He held Roark's head to his chest and looked to see if his arms or legs were broken, or if there was blood anywhere. He seemed to be fine.

A cough. Roark coughed again and slowly opened his eyes.

"Djoser?"

"Yes, Imhotep, I am here." What had he just said? Imhotep? What was happening?

"Riley? My love."

"Yes, Roark. I'm here. Are you all right? I thought—"

"I'm fine. A little woozy. Help me up."

Riley helped him to his feet He kept one arm under his shoulder for support, his hand tight around his waist.

"It has happened," Roark stated grimly.

"What? What has happened? I don't get it. There was a blackout, an earthquake or some—" He stopped himself, looking around the chamber. Both sarcophagi were open, the covers split and lying broken on the floor. The coptic jars and pedestals were smashed into pieces, as if dashed violently to the floor. Had the earthquake been that powerful?

"Two thousand years. Two thousand years I have waited for you, my love—my Pharaoh."

"Pharaoh? What are you talking abo—" Riley's vision

161

blurred. He staggered with Roark still draped over his shoulder. "Roark, I… help me."

Roark gripped him tightly and steadied him. "Rest on this." He leaned Riley against the opened sarcophagus. "Be calm. Let the memories return."

Riley rested both of his hands on the open tomb, noticing that it was empty. His head aching, he closed his eyes.

The memories came in a series of waves, washing over him. Assaulting him. Egypt. The Nile. The palace. Imhotep.

He clutched onto the hard tomb, crying out nonsensical words. He felt arms around him; he clutched at Roark.

Imhotep. The faces merged into one: Imhotep-Roark.

He saw them together in bed. In Egypt. In the palace. Who was he?

Djoser. Imhotep-Roark called him "Djoser. My Pharaoh." Yes!

He was Djoser, pharaoh of Egypt.

Imhotep was his vizier. His lover.

They were together.

He remembered. He remembered it all.

His eyes opened. Emerald ones met his.

Imhotep. Roark.

"Yes, my love, we are together after these two thousand years."

"How? What have you done, Imhotep?"

"I will explain as best I can. If you will remember, I studied medicine, healing, and the magical arts. I discovered that the god, Ptah, was in truth, my father. My mother, Sekhmet, had always told me it was so. And after years of prayer and sacrifice, my father came to me. I told him of our love and of my death-bed promise to you that we would be together again forever."

Riley looked at him in recognition. "I remember your promise as I lay there breathing my last breaths."

"Ptah gave me the scroll of immortality, because I was his son and half-divine. But I pleaded with him for your immortality as well, for I did not want to live if I could not be with you."

Riley's eyes misted and he held Roark's hand.

"Ptah finally relented and told me there was a way, but that it would cost me dearly. I agreed to whatever it was." He stopped, seeming to not want to continue.

Riley squeezed his hand. "What is it you sacrificed for me? What did you give him? You must tell me."

Roark's eyes clouded as well, and the look of unfettered love he gave Riley would have melted the coldest of hearts."My life," he said. "I must give up the rest of my remaining life on Earth. The magic to be performed required me to bury myself alongside you in your crypt." He paused.

Riley his breath, not wanting him to continue but needing to hear it all.

"Alive," Roark finally said. "The coptic jars would be the vessels which would hold our souls until at an unspecified time in the future they would be rejoined. Your soul had already been released to the ether and had to be regained, something only Ptah was capable of, and it could take many years… or never. I would never know when—or if—he had success until I awoke. My sacri—my role would be the offering of myself. My soul was to be stored in the jar until it could be joined with yours."

Riley had to ask. "Do you know how many more years you would have lived?"

"Yes. Ptah told me, for he wanted me to know what I was giving up."

"How long?"

"He told me I would have a long life… fifty-three more years."

Riley dropped his head.

"I would have given up a thousand years for you. My life meant nothing to me without you. You were—you are my life! My pharaoh, my love… my left-field-playing baseball player."

Riley raised his head to Roark, a slight smile quirked at the corner of his mouth. His voice cracked as he spoke. "And I would have done the same for you, my vizier, my professor, my… Indiana Jones."

The two men shared a moment of divine love, knowing that in the depths of their souls what each said was true.

"I have one question," Riley said. "Why do we have memories of both our lives? It's weird remembering being the Pharaoh of Egypt."

"And that, my dear love, I do not know the answer to.

Perhaps one day Ptah will appear and tell us."

"I think that visit from my... father-in-law? I can do without. But as long as I have you, I can handle anything. I assume you're going to marry me?"

"You assume correctly. You will have me for eternity."

"Really? Eternity?"

"That is what the incantation says. Of course, it may be relative to the Egyptian definition of eternity."

"Uh huh. And yep, I lied. I have a hundred more questions, the first one being: how do we get out of here?"

"If you will recall, I was the architect for your pyramid. And I do remember the right configuration of touching the stones for our exit."

"Great. And if no one's in this sarcophagus," Riley indicated the empty tomb. "What or who's in the other one?"

"You don't know?"

"Well, I kind of do. But I need to see this for myself." He went to the open tomb. Roark stood behind him, remaining silent.

"Oh no..." Riley began to cry. He slid down the side of the tomb and rested his forehead against it and weeped.

Roark put his hands on Riley's shoulders. "It was long ago, Riley. History. I would not have changed a thing."

Riley sobbed until he could no longer; Roark kept hold and waited.

Riley rose at last, wiping at his tear-stained face. "It must have been horrible for you."

"I had you," Roark said simply.

Riley stared at the mummified corpse of his own body and at the skeletal remains of Roark… Imhotep. The bone-arms clutched tightly around his tattered, cloth-covered body, locked in an embrace of death.

Riley dragged his eyes away and met Roark's. "Do you still love me like you did then—two thousand years ago?"

"Even more."

Riley hauled him to him, one more sob escaping his lips. "I love you." He kissed Roark tenderly. "Now let's get out of here."

They retraced their steps, and as Roark/Imhotep had assured him knew the correct configuration of pressing stone blocks to release them from the chamber.

There was no one in the vast outer chamber, no tour groups or stragglers.

"Well, since we're immortal we can do whatever we want, right? No plans; just hanging out… making love," Riley said.

"Remember what I said about the Egyptian definition of immortal. It may be different than ours. We may not be. Time will tell."

"So you're saying maybe would we should live everyday like it's our last?"

"I am."

"Then where to next, Indy."

"Wherever your heart desires, my baseball-playing pharaoh."

ABOUT THE AUTHOR

Lance Taubold is the recipient of the IBPA Ben Franklin Award for BEST FIRST NON-FICTION for ON TWO FRONTS.. He has been an entertainer for 25 years, performing at the MET Opera, on Broadway and on television for 5 years on the soap opera "General Hospital." As a writer he has written for Envy Man magazine, both as a fiction writer and book reviewer. His first novel RIPPER A LOVE STORY was written with author Richard Devin.

Taubold is the author of the gay, paranormal romance series: ZODIAC LOVERS BOOKS 1-5.

Taubold has been a contributor to all of the award-winning NEVER FEAR horror anthologies, the UNCHARTED WORLDS-XENO ENCOUNTERS sci-fi anthology and has romance stories in ROMANTIC TIMES: VEGAS, and THE HAUNTED WEST. His next release is the gay romance, murder mystery MAGIC, MURDER AND MISTLETOE. He is currently writing a paranormal romance series with New York Times Bestselling author Heather Graham.

Never Fear Series

Indie Book Award Winner

New York Times bestselling authors, Heather Graham, F. Paul Wilson, Jon Land, Michael Stackpole, Matthew Costello, William F. Nolan and award-winning, master story tellers bring the best in tales of horror.

Never Fear
Shh... Something's Coming...

Never Fear – Phobias
Everyone Fears Something

Never Fear - Christmas Terrors
He Sees You When You're Sleeping...

Never Fear - The Tarot
Do You Really Want To Know...

Never Fear – Apocalypse
The End is Near...

RT Booklovers Presents: The Haunted West

Written especially for RT Booklovers, best-selling and award-winning authors Diana Gabaldon, Heather Graham, Virginia Henley, Kat Martin, Katherine Neville, Bobbi Smith, Tina Wainscott, Tina DeSalvo and more... take you on a time-traveling, spellbinding journey through America's sprawling West.

The Haunted West, Volume 1

The Haunted West, Volume 2

Romantic Times: Vegas

The Excelsior Hotel and Casino.in Las Vegas is the setting of these magical stories of romance. For decades the towering hotel has been the subject of incredible stories and rumors. Bestselling authors, Christina Skye, Heather Graham, Tina DeSalvo and a story by the Lady of Barrow, Kathryn Falk will take you deep into the heart of those, in the past, present and future... who roam the halls of the Excelsior in search of that perfect love.

Volume 1

Volume 2

Volume 3

Heather Graham's Christmas Treasures

Heather Graham's Haunted Treasures

Presented together for the first time, New York Times Bestselling Author, Heather Graham brings back three out-of-print Christmas classics that are sure to inspire, amaze, and warm your heart.

Heather Graham's Christmas Treasures also available in **Invoke Books Dyslexic Friendly**

New York Times Bestselling Author, Heather Graham brings back three tales of paranormal love and adventure.

The Third Hour

Winner of the USA Best Book Award - Thrillers

The Third Hour is an original spin on the religious-thriller genre, incorporating elements of science fiction along with the religious angle. Its strength lies in this originality, combined with an interesting take on real historical figures, who are made a part of the experiment at the heart of the novel.

Ripper – A Love Story

Prince Edward Albert Victor, The Duke of Clarence is Queen Victoria's favorite grandson and the most eligible bachelor in England. Coren Butler has captured his heart in the perfect Cinderella story. A dream come true. Then the nightmare begins.

Uncharted Worlds: Xeno Encounters

Uncharted Worlds—an exciting new speculative fiction series featuring bestselling and award-winning authors. Ten mind-boggling adventures include tales of ancient aliens, other worlds, and imagined futures.

On Two Fronts

IBPA Silver Medal Best Non-Fiction Award Winner

When two unlikely friends are separated by war, they must learn to cope with the effect it will have on their lives, their futures, and their relationship.

Bad Attitude/Diamond in the Rough

Bad Attitude Meet bad boy, undercover state trooper Reid Cameron. Meet Polly Sweet, the woman who is about to be his downfall. In order to catch a jewel thief, Cameron wants to use Polly's house, and he comes up with a plan, whereby they play at being lovers. But when the first play-acted kiss happens, neither one is ready for the feelings that kiss ignites or for the consequences that ensue.

Has this bad boy finally met his match? How Bad is Too Bad?

Diamond In The Rough-Detective Dan Murdock is on a dangerous stakeout, when advice columnist, Millie Gordon unwittingly shows up on the scene, putting them both in danger. To save her from possibly being shot when the mobsters arrive, Murdock jumps into Millie's car and throws himself over her to protect her, little realizing that the real danger starts when their bodies come together.

Romance and action are the name of the game in this two-in-one duo from bestselling author Doris Parmett.

Calendar Girl

Fate, it seems, has derailed destiny… and found a love for all time. Tina Wainscott weaves a tale you'll not soon forget.

Family

Matthew Costello's widely acclaimed post-apocalyptic thriller, comes to it's amazing conclusion.

Treasures and Pleasures

A Collection of Romantic Novellas from the bestselling author Bobbi Smith.

Shadows in the Big Easy

Bouchercon Presents stories by up and coming Teen Writing Contest winners in this mystery anthology.

Stop Saying Yes – Negotiate!

Stop Saying Yes - Negotiate! is the perfect "on the go" guide for all negotiations. Fortune 500 Companies world-wide send out their teams of negotiators with copies tucked away in briefcases and notebooks... maybe you should too?

Do You Want To Be An Actor?

101 Answers To Your Questions About Breaking Into The Biz from people who know, Casting Directors, Producers, Directors and Agents tell it like it is.

Zodiac Lovers Series

In this series of romantic, gay, paranormal stories tales of love lost, love found, and love to last for eternity will fill your heart with awe and your eyes with tears.

Zodiac Lovers 1: Aquarius, Pisces, Aries

Zodiac Lovers 2: Taurus, Gemini, Cancer

Zodiac Lovers 3: Leo, Virgo, Libra

Zodiac Lovers 4: Scorpio, Sagittarius, Capricorn

Zodiac Lovers 5: Cetus, Ophiuchus